PRAISE FOR D.O.

'A brave and original writer'
- Joseph Kertes, winner of the National Jewish Book Award for *Gratitude*

'A starkly brutal existential journey into power, guilt, identity, bureaucracy and the darkest corners of the human soul.'
- Michael Mirolla, author of *Berlin*

'This is our world turned on its head, and wonderfully writ. Astonishing.'
- Linda Spalding, author of *Who Named the Knife*, co-editor of *Brick Magazine*

'Riveting, horrific, poetic brilliance.'
- Michael Turner, author of *The Pornographers Poem*

'Undeniably powerful, a thought-provoking book that lingers in the mind.'
- *Winnipeg Free Press*

'*Whispers the Missing Child* is a remarkable book full of dark intense imagery and strange beauty. Nearer a poem than a novel, it stays with the reader like the haunting it describes.'
- A.L Kennedy

JEW

Also by D.O. Dodd

THE HOSTAGE TAKER

WHISPERS THE MISSING CHILD

JEW

D.O. Dodd

NO EXIT PRESS

First published in the UK in 2010
This paperback edition published in 2011 by
No Exit Press, P.O.Box 394,
Harpenden, Herts, AL5 1XJ
www.noexit.co.uk

A CIP catalogue record for this book is available from the British Library.

ISBN 978-1-84243-399-7 (paperback)

978-1-84243-605-9 (kindle)
978-1-84243-606-6 (ePub)
978-1-84243-607-3 (PDF)

2 4 6 8 10 9 7 5 3 1

Drawings by Claire Weissman Wilks

Typeset by Avocet Typeset, Chilton, Aylesbury, Bucks

Printed and bound by
CPI Group (UK) Ltd, Croydon, CR0 4YY

For M

The plague, like a great fire, if a few houses only are
contiguous where it happens, can only burn a few houses;
or if it begins in a single, or, as we call it, a lone house,
can only burn that lone house where it begins.
But if it begins in a close-built town or city and gets a head,
there its fury increases: it rages over the whole place,
and consumes all it can reach.

—Daniel Defoe

CHAPTER 1

He found himself awake in blackness, his eyes coming open uneasily, as though his lashes were webbed together.

His cheek appeared flattened. He inched his head sideways to relieve the pressure on his nose and lips. They felt engorged, swollen out of shape. He discovered that his tongue was extended, and worked it back into his mouth.

It was difficult to move his dry eyes, to move his body against the chilled, hard smoothness that pinned his legs, back, chest, stomach, groin…

His breathing was hoarse and amplified in the close space. It lingered to return to him; the invasive stench of refuse left out in the sun for months on end.

He tried lifting his head. It butted against something above him, knocking him back down. The movement intensified sensation in his panging ear.

The reek was now a stain in his lungs, urging him to action. Incited, he took notice of his arms, bent and stretching away from his shoulders. The realization that he was trapped tingled and fluttered through him.

Fright cut short his breath, surging toward panic, but his body, weak and stuck as it was, could not shift.

He struggled to nudge his left foot free, his toes were

bare. His right foot, jammed at the ankle, would not budge.

He became aware of light – pale white, filtered vaguely green and pink – as he noticed that his left arm was bare, that his entire body must be naked.

Why naked?

Then came the drone of buzzing, as though from beyond a wall.

He tried moving his fingers on each hand. The fingers on his right hand were pinned between two cool, smooth surfaces.

As he stirred the fingers of his left hand, they felt something mossy, cold and dusty dry. He rubbed the material between his fingertips, warming the texture to memory. The strands separated, and curled around his finger. Hair.

As he struggled, twisting and pushing, straining his muscles, he felt hard edges intrude upon his body, attempting to tangle with him as they shifted woodenly to become displaced.

The light closed over in one space and opened in bits in another. The drone of buzzing became louder.

He felt what must be a foot with his foot. Sole to sole. Frigid.

The muscles in his neck went taut as he turned his head to see a stopped living thing unto itself, an orb, trained on him with vacuous intent.

Then – as though bared by a shadowed hint of dawn – a face became apparent.

A woman with her breathless mouth open. Stalled.

It was then that he found the strength.

He thrust his left hand upward. It smacked against flesh, his fingernails digging in, then plucking out, his hand pawing around, finding an edge, his fingers searching to discover space, the shallow depth of a hole.

The severe meeting of shapes beneath his back was atrocious.

He turned on his side, and pushed with his right hand, his arm forced straight, trying to bend his elbow in the confines, inching through the indefinite outline of the mass above him.

He squirmed with his shoulder, and kicked down to find a place for his feet, working his way into the irregular wedge of a gap between what he now knew to be bodies.

The strain had brought on a sweat, and the warmth of his body smeared against cold flesh to all sides of him.

Again, he reached up with his left hand; his fingers – while fearing touch – frantically hunted for space, and found a small, dry hollow, crowned by rough edges. Teeth.

He drew back his fingers, his elbow striking something bone-hard behind skin.

He pushed with his right hand, his fingers slipping, contours of the bodies becoming plainer to him now, his mind anxious to deny what was being touched.

A shoulder? A buttock? A breast? A knee? An elbow? All inflexible.

He scrambled in fits and starts, his throat making sounds.

Noise mounted in his head.

He was almost vertical.

He shoved with held breath, squeezing through the unwilling weight of bodies, while labouring to raise his left hand higher, his fingers desperately skimming over each cold surface.

Out. Out. Out.

Where?

With his head turned upward on an awkward angle – allowed by the settling pressure of the bodies – his right eye saw light. An illumination of grey with moving black specks, as though wavering and sparkling darkly at once.

He feared that he might go mad, and raged against the weight on all sides of him.

Gasping a breath, he held it trapped, and pushed with his feet and knees, pressed with his arms, elbows, hips and back.

At once, he stopped.

He retched, the pressure in his nostrils blooming.

With his left arm stretched upward, fixed above his head, and the right bent at his side, he could not wipe his eyes.

His fingertips, searching around obstructions, soon found unencumbered space. Cool, open air.

He struggled until he felt that he had gained an adequate vertical position. His heels and toes pried into edges, seeking a depression to support each step of his climb.

He was slipping free of the bodies; sweat greased everything to all sides of him. Hair matted to his forehead. Right elbow squat close to his side, he worked to extend that arm, to reach like the other.

He did not stop struggling until both arms were above his head, and the top of his scalp felt fresh air.

It was easier now, with the bodies for support, to rise inches at a time.

Flies batted off his forehead, off his nose, lips and ears.

Again, he retched, this time on account of sensation.

Water filled his eyes, so that he had to swipe away the blur.

The spasm of a dry heave struck with such violence that he feared it might tear open his throat.

Buckled forward, with his torso still buried, he was stuck.

The bodies now seemed set on holding him to them, on preventing him from breaking loose, as he braced his hands against the cruel geometry of hard flesh to pry himself out of the hole.

Struggling as though in concert with his struggling, the bodies clung on, then eventually, in giving increments, released their grip.

He found it an arduously uneven task to stand, yet did not want to crouch with his hands touching dead flesh.

His knees trembled. His calf muscles flinched spasmodically.

A living man atop a heap of skin and bones.

Dizzy to the point of tipping toward unconsciousness, he knew that he had to walk or faint away, yet could not find the strength to take a single step.

The bottoms of his feet were unbearably sensitive. Itchy.

Again, his stomach knotted with revulsion.

He rubbed the tears away with the back of his arm, his

head hanging. Then he raised his eyes to glance around for signs of life.

Chest clutched by a sob, he cupped his hands over his mouth and nostrils.

A grey sky overhead.

Two sheds nearby, a wide smear of black leading from the closest shed to the pile of bodies.

His knees continued shivering where he stood. The knobby shapes beneath his feet made him shift for balance. He thought of leaping into the air, to get clear of the corpses, but then imagined coming down.

He could not convince himself to step across this surface. He was naked, the air cool on his skin. He was relieved, yet terrified.

Was he free of this horror or a living part of it?

Flies.

What was this horror?

He tried not to look down.

The drone was deafening as he shut his eyes, and took his first step.

He continued, carefully stepping in bare feet across dead bodies.

He tried spitting the flies away, weakly swatting at them, snorting them out of his nostrils.

He opened his eyes. Where to step? On a back? A stomach? He avoided the rigid faces, the hands, the feet. What not to offend?

That sound of buzzing like a million tiny engines powered by mere drops of blood.

He slipped on the hard incline of a leg and fell on his backside, thudded against a child's head, which bobbed beneath him, his hand having grabbed for the safety of a woman's face.

So many spaces to lose his fingers in.

His yelping was its own erratic scramble as he rolled down the side of the mound, banging his knees and elbows against offence after offence.

He hit the ground, and hurried off, stumbling over.

He collapsed, crawled, shot a look back, scurrying away with his fingers digging into earth while he sat.

The pile of bodies was fifteen feet high.

He was free, yet he was confounded and horrified.

The drone of flies distantly filled his ears. Not so loud now. Regardless, he spat and spat. If he breathed through his nose, the flies went in.

He hawked and spat, trying to clear his tongue of the flies already drowned in his saliva. If he opened his mouth, the flies entered, troubled the back of his throat.

He kept hawking and spitting

Swatting, he slid away another two metres. Then stopped.

Stopped dead still with his heart alight.

There was movement in the heap.

Another body coming to life?

A noise of encouragement in his throat. He made a motion to stand, was on his feet, when he saw a long thin tail slink after the movement.

He stopped himself.

He faltered, plunked back down and frantically checked his toes and fingers. He felt at his ears for ragged pieces. Nothing seemed tattered.

When he regarded the pile, he noticed other movements, which, again, brightened his outlook.

The grey fur and the flick of a tail.

He had come out of the centre of it. He had escaped, yet he had no idea why the pile of bodies was there, why he had been in it. Had he been dead? Or simply left for dead?

He glanced over his shoulder. Two small buildings.

Free from the abomination, he had no idea where or who he was.

A black trail led back to the first shed; marks gouged in the dirt. Flies were clouded along the smear, settling and rising in restless swirls.

Inside the shed, the floor was tacky. The feeling made him want to curl his toes upward.

There were clothes on the ground, rags bundled toward the corners. A smell in his nostrils came to him from the clothes, the same smell as in the heap.

He wiped at his nose. But the stench would not be dispelled. He squeezed his nostrils shut, held them that way. He was hungry, yet he was dizzy and appalled.

Again, he retched, then made a shuddering sound with his lips.

Hung on a number of hooks in the wall were clothes of a cleaner variety: a black shirt and black trousers, a jacket with shimmering insignias on the sleeves.

He swayed for balance as he carefully pulled on the trousers and fastened the hasp. Drawing up the zipper, he noticed his thin fingers, their sickly whiteness, the tremble in them. There was no profit in taking more notice, yet he could not help but wonder if he might be ill.

A disorienting buzzing rose in his ear. He shut his eyes and braced one arm against the rough wall, until the upswelling passed.

He slowly fit his arms into the sleeves of the shirt, fastened the row of buttons, and pulled on the jacket.

Then he saw the wide leather belt with the holster. He lifted it down. It was heavy. He admired the weight of it, knew what it was made for, how to buckle it around his waist.

He was not shivering so much now. He felt almost calm, confident.

There was movement against his toe. He flinched, turned his foot on an angle. A rat, sniffing at him.

He backed away, while the rat chewed at a shapeless clump stuck to the floor.

There were boots stood toward one of the walls. He put them on. They were half a size too big for him.

To his left, there was a door. A man's sound came to him, perhaps a mumble from sleep, followed by the creaking of bed springs.

He froze and was sweating at once; the living gap that was his stomach contracted.

He found that his hand was already on the holster, that his fingers had unfastened the catch and the abrasive handle was gripped in his palm, the weighty revolver swept clean of the holster, the barrel pointed toward the room.

The soles of his boots stuck and released as he

approached the door, and quietly pressed it open.

Through the crack, he saw a man on the bed, sleeping on his side, his arm across the chest of a naked woman with snipped-short black hair. The woman was lying on her back, her arms stiff at her sides, while she stared at the ceiling.

The naked man's feet were stained black-red.

He crept into the room, and the stickiness beneath his boots became pronounced. His boots made a sound that woke the naked man, who rose up on one elbow to look directly at him.

The man stared with surprise and then with confusion, as the man could have been his twin.

The woman took no notice, but kept staring at the ceiling, as though pressed into that pose, anchored dutifully to her place on the bed.

The naked man said something that could not be understood as he sat fully up to ready himself. His tone was demanding, yet reasonable, as though engaged in bargaining with someone familiar to him. He outstretched his hand for the gun.

This gesture alone was sufficient to set him off. Where he had merely meant to tighten his grip on the revolver, he was startled when it exploded in his hand, the noise blasting attentiveness through his head. It swelled out from the centre to echo and ring.

The revolver dropped, as the naked man fell back onto the stained mattress, which creaked and shifted beneath the woman who did not change her expression or position.

Pressed back against the mattress, the naked man watched him, stared at him. The naked man quietly said a word, a name, barely audible in his ringing ears.

He noticed that his fingertips, where they had been holding the revolver, had warmed from white to dusty pink.

In the second shed, he discovered a lidded, silver serving tray perched on a table, slapped together from grey planks. He raised the rounded lid to uncover slices of bread, meats and cheese prettily arranged. There were green grapes and plump strawberries circling the ornate border.

Alongside the tray, there was a silver thermos.

He ate the bread and meat, his eyes searching around, his ears intently listening, as his throat made noises while he chewed.

At one point, in a fit of furious swallowing, he choked on a wad of bread, but managed to get it dislodged.

He twisted the lid off the thermos. Inside, the fluid was

warm. It smelled like coffee. He gulped it down, then devoured a few grapes and strawberries, walked back out into the yard with sweetness in his mouth.

Alive.

All around the heap of bodies, there was sand bulldozed into hills, as though the site had once been an excavation pit. There was a road beyond the mound that stretched across a straight, desolate plain of land, where small orange wavers were evident in the distance.

He found a black sedan at the back of the second shed. It was polished, gleaming.

By the driver's door, he was struck by sickness and bent forward, vomiting.

He could smell the scent of the naked man whose body he had dragged from the shed. It had taken him some time to deposit it on the pile of bodies that was more of an oddity to him now that he was no longer a factor in it.

When he straightened, he saw, beyond his reflection, a hat resting on the driver's seat. He opened the door and lifted out the hat. Doing so, he noticed keys dangling in the ignition.

He went back into the second shed, where he washed his face and hands in the trickle of coffee that remained in the thermos.

Back outside, he regarded the bodies, then inclined his attention up at the grey sky. A fat raindrop hit him squarely in the face, just beneath his lips. He jerked spasmodically, and wiped it away.

Soon, patterings tapped at the ground everywhere, as a single cloud let loose its burden.

He climbed into the sedan, and watched the rain beat down upon the windshield. Then he turned the key, engaged the engine, switched on the windshield wipers for a clearer view, and drove away.

At a roadblock, a man in a uniform held up his hand, while stepping forward from a makeshift wooden shelter.

He slowed the car, but then the man – inquisitively leaning to peer in the window – waved the car on.

He sped up.

It was necessary to keep moving, to find another place that was far from the one he could still catch a glimpse of in his rear-view mirror.

Military vehicles were pulled off on the sides of the roads. Soldiers, lingering near, suspended their conversations or laughter, to straighten and salute him.

Fires burned in the dusty fields, as soldiers worked tossing in bodies.

He passed through two more roadblocks, and, at each one, he was briskly waved ahead without question.

A kilometre beyond the final roadblock, he entered a small village with low wooden buildings on either side of a dirt street.

Words and symbols were painted on many of the buildings.

People walking along the thoroughfare stopped when they saw the shiny black sedan, their faces curiously nervous.

He pulled over in front of a building with one window cracked and the other boarded over, and climbed out of the car to feel that the burst of rain had stopped. The heat had intensified to such a degree that he felt it might scorch the top of his head should he remove his hat.

There was not another car to be seen.

Stepping up onto the building's wooden landing, his boots banged loudly. A man coming out the door froze and held the door open, his head bowed.

Inside, there were three tables with groups of men seated at them.

He stood at the bar, and said: "I've just come from a pile of bodies." His words, the only ones to have entered his mind, sounded foreign in his own ears.

The room turned dead quiet, the ensuing silence mounting to a daze.

The barman laid a small cup of coffee on the bar, and nodded, his eyes steady and watchful.

He turned to see the faces trying not to notice him.

Only one table was any different from the rest. Seated near the door, a man began muttering to the others. Then, the man stood. Another man reached out for the man who had stood, but the standing man yanked his sleeve away.

"It can't be him," said the other man.

"You've come in," said the man, stating a name. "How is that possible? Into our special place." The man clumsily drew nearer, while studying his face. "It is you." Again, the name.

He took a drink from the cup that had been offered.

"A sudden change of faith." The man laughed meanly, his eyes on the uniform. "And quickly risen in the ranks."

"Who are you?"

The man sneered. "Who am I?"

"Yes."

The man spat on his boots, then eyed his holster. "You can have your friends shoot me now. Or you. You can do it yourself."

"Why would I do that?"

"You're all meek kindness then," the man said with sarcasm, checking over his shoulder for proof of shared sentiment.

He raised the cup to his lips again, and drank. At once, he felt light-headed. And he knew it would only get worse. He turned to the barman. "Is there something here to eat?"

"Of course." The barman nodded deeply, respectfully. "Food, you mean. Yes," he said, backing away.

He felt a hand on his shoulder. When he turned, he saw that the man – his face now filled with wonder – was clutching him with a grip that seemed puny.

"How is this possible?" the man quietly asked. "How?"

He shook his head, while searching the man's tormented eyes.

"Is that what you are, a Jew?" the man whispered despondently. Then, he shouted the same words again.

A few men rose from their tables and headed for the door.

"I don't know." He studied the man's hand, then sighed, for he had intended to go unnoticed.

"You don't know."

"Does it matter?"

Tight, low laughter came from the tables, only to be broken by a woman's scream in the street. The men at the tables ignored it. The man removed his hand, turning his head to face the door.

He was the only one to move. On instinct, he stepped toward the entrance, and opened it.

Outside, across the road, two soldiers down an alleyway were bent over a woman, shoving her into the mud. Others, in civilian clothes, stood by watching with peculiar interest.

"Stop," he called, fully pushing through the door, his voice barely loud enough. He cleared his throat.

The two soldiers looked at him. Frozen in action. Their faces were jeering. Their hands were on the woman's arm or gripping her long black hair so that her head was pulled on a taut angle.

"Leave her," he said, and the soldiers took their hands from the woman. He watched the soldiers straighten reluctantly, confused, yet prepared for further instruction.

The woman ran off with a surge like something wild let loose.

He took a good look at the soldiers, who now appeared mystified by the situation.

"Should we shoot her?" one soldier asked, gesturing after the woman.

"No."

They said nothing more of it, and he noticed how the sun was on the street, while he and the soldiers were in shadows cast from the buildings.

He went back inside to find a plate set down on the bar. Boiled eggs sprinkled with salt. He ate both eggs, and asked for another, pointing at the plate.

Two more were quickly given over.

The room remained respectfully hushed.

Occasionally, he checked over his shoulder, patiently watching the men who watched him. They did not move an inch. Their tongues could not have been stiller.

"Do you know who I am?" he finally asked the men at the table nearest him.

"We know," called the agitated man by the door. "No need to brag about it."

CHAPTER 2

The two soldiers were slowly moving around his car, checking it over with interest. They caught sight of him as he stepped out of the building. One looked at the other, before they approached him, and saluted.

"Where do I go from here?" he asked, straightening his belt.

"We'll take you there," said the younger soldier, hoisting a rifle strap higher on his shoulder.

They led him down off the wooden landing, where they walked in the centre of the dirt road, oblivious to the stray movements of other people.

"Did you have a comfortable journey?" asked the younger soldier, who seemed to be of a more pleasant nature than the other.

He thought about this question, wondering on an answer.

After giving no reply, he was not bothered again. He stared ahead, his boots striding, his uncertain haste mistaken for a pledge to duty. He guessed that he was being taken to make an impression on someone.

At the end of the town, they stepped into a low, well-preserved building with a sign marking it as the post office.

A balding man in a uniform with insignias on its sleeve

was seated behind a desk. Two filing cabinets stood as sentinels to either side of him. The man rose from his chair, said what might have been one of their names, and saluted.

He did not return the salute, but merely stood there.

The room was of interest to him, for there was a makeshift cell toward the back. He glanced at the two soldiers, who took this for a gesture of dismissal, and left at once.

Indicating the chair, the balding officer said: "Please, have a seat, commander."

He did not sit. "Please," he said, "explain to me what is going on here."

The balding officer squinted, his mouth made a strange shape of itself, as his eyes glanced at his desktop in a gesture of compliance. "How do you mean, sir?"

He said nothing. He felt the need to count the insignias on the man's sleeve, and then count the greater number on his own.

"Tell me." He leaned forward, stammered by a clutch of weakness, and was made to brace his hands on the edge of the desk.

The man's eyebrows crowded together. Lines etched into his forehead. "I... don't..."

He sat back into the chair, almost fell, his descent making a great deal of noise, as he had unwittingly kicked the front of the desk with his boots.

The man in the uniform flinched.

Behind him, the door opened. He turned in reflex, straining to see the two soldiers rush back in.

The balding officer raised his hand to the soldiers.

The younger one nodded and backed away, the older one was more reluctant, his mind and body banded by mechanisms of mistrust.

He stared at the man behind the desk.

"We were expecting you yesterday," the balding officer indicated.

He simply stared. "There were hundreds of bodies."

"Yes. I expect."

"You know how this happened?"

"Yes, yes, of course." The officer stood and stepped hurriedly out from behind the desk. He gestured toward his own chair with both hands. "Please."

He stood and went around the desk, carefully sat in the chair that was already warm. He joined his hands on the desktop. They were regaining warmth, almost fully coloured, moving from warm to hot.

"We were told to expect new orders for the district, sir."

"Orders?"

"Yes. Considering the developing predicament," the officer said, newly doubtful of his own abilities. He glanced out the window, then regarded him again.

"I would like something done about those bodies. There was a woman in a bed."

"Yes," confirmed the officer. "I have heard from someone." He said a name, averted his eyes, shifted them toward the desktop where two files lay opened. Women's names were printed on the tabs.

The files contained photographs where flash bulbs had been used in confined places.

"At Relief Camp 7," the officer said. "The bodies will be burned. The woman, too. You have no need to worry, sir."

"Worry?"

"You don't worry. I know," the officer said timidly, but more toward gruff rudeness.

"I want the bodies brought here."

The officer's expression inclined toward change. "The woman?"

"All of them."

"To this town, sir?"

"YES." He startled even himself with this outburst, every nerve in his body shocked to life, so that his hands trembled. He tightened them into a fist to hold steady.

At once, the two soldiers re-entered. The younger one must have been only eighteen. The older one was in his twenties and had a rough face. He kept his head tilted on an angle, while he watched wordlessly.

"The commander would like the bodies from Relief Camp 7 brought here."

"Here?" asked the younger soldier, his finger pointing to the floor.

"To this town," said the balding officer.

He shut his eyes and listened. It would be effortless to drift off, to fall into a calm sleep. In darkness, he remembered the black trail leading to the pile of bodies, and opened his eyes.

"In the fields?"

"No, inside."

"There's not a building large enough, sir."

"I want them in the houses."

"The houses?" The younger soldier looked from him to the balding officer, who was standing off to the side, as though wanting to avoid the proceedings. The younger soldier wiped at his nose. "I mean, I'm not certain I understand, sir."

"The homes." From where he was seated behind the desk of the post office, he stared at the younger soldier. The look on the older soldier's face was making him angry. "Back where they belong."

"In the truck, sir?"

He continued staring, and shifted his jaw.

"Yes?" asked the younger soldier.

"Yes."

The younger soldier knew better than to pose another question.

His eyes were back on the photographs. Three men around a naked woman with a black hood over her head. One of the men had been laughing, his lips pursed jovially, as though he were saying something precious into the camera.

"Sir?" asked the older soldier.

"Yes?" He looked up.

"You have some markings here." He raised his hand, and touched his own cheek. "And here." The older soldier moved his hand to his forehead.

He quietly wiped at his forehead with his fingertips, while the older soldier watched him with keen interest. The gritty texture of dirt soon crumbled to the desktop. He wondered what it was, and brushed it away.

"One of the women will give you a bath," said the balding officer, making a joke of it.

The younger soldier laughed, but the older soldier was unsatisfied.

"Leave me alone now," he said, wanting to concentrate on the photographs.

And the three others saluted, and left him to himself.

That night, he felt the need to wander off, beyond the edge of town.

Further out in the darkness there were three fires visible. Only in the nearest one, perhaps a half kilometre away, could he discern the shadows of soldiers lifting what might have been bodies.

Occasionally, there seemed to be the white fluttering of wings, which he soon realized were pages from books being flung into the air, descending, then rising to hover alit.

He looked toward the sky. A crescent moon shining bright. A single star. It made him wonder why all of this was beneath it.

Behind him, the low wooden buildings and houses to either side of the road were quiet and removed. He sensed that – inside those structures – people were talking about him, giving speculation to what not even he could verify.

What was he meant to do here, for the focus appeared to be entirely on him?

When he faced the wall of blackness again, with the three various-sized flames glowing at particular distances, he felt a reluctant thrill. The air was cool. It was summertime, he suspected.

Refreshed, he turned to head back, and was faced by a woman, standing no more than five feet away, watching him.

At first, he thought she might be dead on her feet; so still did she stand there. She had long, coal-black hair that was parted in the middle, and equally dark eyebrows and lashes. Her face was oval with a full serious mouth and a pronounced dimple in her chin. Pink flecks were scattered on her cheeks, as though from a rash that had healed. A strand of hair hung toward the front of her face, revealing the entirety of her left ear. She was holding her hands outstretched, and in each of her palms there was a bagel.

He watched the woman's face, while she studied his, and he slowly began to feel that he might know her.

"I made these for you," she said, observing him with large brown eyes. "You like them, yes? They're for helping me earlier today."

He took the warm bagels from her. She had long fingers. The feminine sight of them filled him with soft wonder.

"You're always helping me, it seems."

The bagels grew warmer in his hands.

Sweeping her gaze over his face, the woman then turned and walked away.

He watched her stroll off, her long skirt swaying with her stride.

How am I always helping you, he thought to ask.

The two soldiers, smoking outside the post office, gave the woman some unkind attention as she passed.

When he arrived at the post office, thinking to say something to them about who the woman might be, he heard the younger soldier remark: "She could be brought to you, sir."

He tried guessing at what the soldier might have meant.

"It's not a problem, sir?"

Not certain of the appropriate response, he nodded.

"We'll arrange her for the new commander," the older soldier remarked to the younger one. "She already knows of his fondness for her." In the lamplight from within, his eyes were cruel and incredible.

The bodies from Relief Camp 7 were scheduled for pickup and transport commencing at 0800 hours. The lists of names had been drawn out from one of the filing cabinets by the balding officer who knew of their exact location.

Each name belonged to a body in the pile.

He thought that by looking through the names he might recognize his own, but they were merely words to him, a list that brought nothing to mind.

Yet, as he continued studying the words, he saw the lines and dots twist, lengthen and arc to form the outline of the heap he had crawled from.

The names of the women were held in his head. They reminded him of the photographs he had reviewed earlier, and he wondered if a certain name might belong to a certain face.

Standing up from his chair, he went to the cabinet in the farthest corner, his eyes avoiding the makeshift cell. He opened the top drawer, and searched in the space where the balding officer had slid away the files in question. He found them from memory, and returned with them to his desk.

Opening the top one, he faced the hooded woman.

He flipped deeper, until encountering the bare face in

the formal photograph taken when the woman had been first apprehended. It was the woman who had given him the bagels. He recalled her words: "You're always helping me, it seems."

The file indicated that the woman had been relocated to here from another town, and assigned to bakery duty.

He took his time going through the photographs of the black-haired woman. After viewing the images, which swirled up turbulence in his mind, it was not so easy to read the words.

He read about her birth and her childhood, her job. She had not married. Other details were sketchy and made him suspect that what he was reading was pure speculation on the part of whoever had written out these supposed facts.

Done with the words, he returned to the particulars of one of the photographs. The woman's arms were held out by her sides. Her feet spaced a wide distance. A wooden device rose to an edge between her legs.

Again, he returned to the words, and read about her family. A dead father, a holy man, accused and eliminated. A mother, thought to be alive, in hiding. He turned the page to study another photograph.

Documents were included outlining the woman's

reaction to the various indignities that were inflicted on her. The methods used were ingeniously vile.

He worked his way toward the bottom of the file, where he came upon something that caused him confusion. The final sheet of paper was the woman's death certificate.

While he was reading over the certificate, which was dated for a time he had no way of authenticating, his fingertip pressed against one of the photographs, making a smear toward the woman's bare, right shoulder.

Glass shattered to his left, and a stream of orange gushed into the room. With a powerful, incinerating whoosh, fire fanned out across the floor.

He stood as the flames shot up and clung to the walls.

The compelling fragrance of gasoline filled his lungs, while the temperature exceeded human threshold.

The path to the door was vaguely clear. As he hurried toward it, he felt the heat intensify in his hair and on his face and the back of the hand that reached for the knob.

The door opened from the other side, the younger officer hurrying to help.

He stepped out to the sputter of machine-gun fire in the darkness.

It was remarkably hot for night. He looked at his arm and saw that his coat sleeve was ablaze. The younger soldier tried patting it out. He pulled off his jacket, and threw it out into the street where it burned in a small pile.

The heat against his back was growing harsh. He stepped down the stairs, as a soldier hurried toward him with a bucket of water, and ran into the post office without giving him notice.

Another soldier arrived with a wide flat tank on his back, and commenced spraying the post office.

More machine-gun fire, soft and feathery.

Men's shouts, rough and halted.

Women's yielding screams.

The two soldiers desperately battled the fire, but their struggle was ineffective. The post office burned in a bright blaze, a fierce, snapping crackle that grew higher and drove him and the three soldiers back, a step at a time.

He turned to look at the houses across the street, the reflection of brilliant orange in the windows. The woman who had given him the bagels that now burned on his desk was standing behind a pane on the second floor. He wondered why the woman remained in the window, why there were not more people in the street.

He called over the soldier with the flat metal tank strapped to his back, and pointed to the windows. "Why don't they come out?"

The soldier with the tank appeared to have no idea how to answer.

"Get them out," he said.

"They're not permitted, sir," the younger soldier spoke up in a voice meant to compete with the roar of flames. "In darkness."

One of the two soldiers unknown to him, the one with the bucket, came over and watched his face.

From down the dirt street, a shadow emerged. The shadow leaned one way, dragging along a burden.

As the shadow neared, it took on the look of the older soldier. In the soldier's other hand, a machine gun was steadied against his hip and pointed toward the sky. When he arrived, he let loose the arm of the body.

"This is him," said the older soldier, spitting on the corpse.

"Who?" he asked, seeing the man who accosted him earlier in the building where he had refreshed himself with coffee and food.

"The one who threw the Molotov cocktail."

"Get the people out of those houses." He turned his head and pointed to the houses next to the post office.

"And shoot them?" asked the older soldier, his mouth bunching up with vengeance.

Caught by surprise, he looked at the older soldier's face. "What?"

"There's only the women left now. This," and he nudged the body on the ground with his boot, "was one of the last of the men." He pointed back into the darkness, down the centre of the road where no houses or buildings showed a single sign of life or light. "The others, the men with him are back there. Silent now, too. They were involved." He straightened the barrel of his machine gun, as though to vouch for its potency.

He looked at the house next to the post office. It was already on fire. "Get them out of there." Again, he pointed.

The older soldier did not move.

"They're not permitted outside at night, sir," put in the younger soldier. "Orders from the supreme commander."

The balding officer hurried into the light of the fire. He was fitting his left arm into his jacket. He looked at the body on the ground, then at the blaze.

"What was saved?" the balding officer wanted to know. "The files?"

The exterior of the house next to the post office was almost entirely engulfed in flames.

He heard a moaning scream from within. A wailing, much like a chant.

No one paid it any mind.

He hurriedly strode toward the house, up the two steps, and kicked open the front door. A woman stood there, halfway down the fiery hallway. Ablaze, she slowly knelt, as though melting, and touched her palms and head against the floor.

His eyebrows and lashes grew dry in the intense heat. At once, his lungs contracted and he coughed violently, and stumbled dizzily.

The wailing scream he had been hearing crackled out as the woman steadily became a ball of flame. In the centre of the flame, the form that had ignited continued shrinking.

The colour of blood in his stinging eyes.

The heat grew greater as the hairs on the backs of his hands contracted. He felt a hand on his shoulder, gently pulling him back. He jerked his shoulder to free it, and the movement brought on a coughing fit.

"Sir," called out the younger soldier, wearily, worried.

He coughed again and kept coughing. There was no way of suppressing it. His eyes ran with tears, blurring the raging colours.

The woman was nothing but fire now, like the house itself. There was no difference.

"Sir?" The voice had taken a step back. Yet a hand reached out and tugged at his shirt. He could not stop himself from leaving the fire.

He wiped at his eyes, and allowed himself to be returned to the other men. While his coughing subsided, he noticed the balding officer staring with misgiving at his face.

"Were the files rescued?" the balding officer asked around.

"No," he answered for all present, his bile-raw throat constricting. Regardless, he wanted to say that word, to somehow penalize the balding officer with the finality of it. He spoke it again: "No."

"In the cabinets?"

"No."

"Nothing?" The balding officer seemed frantic.

"Get the women out of those houses."

"That's impossible, sir, except for the workers."

"Impossible?"

"They're not permitted out after dark. We'll rescue the workers, though. Not to worry."

He shook his head. Again, he shook it. Dumbfounded.

The expression on the balding officer's face turned remarkably plain.

A thought jerked his head. He coughed while he spoke: "Where are the children?"

"They've been sent away. We'll never know now." The officer stared toward the burning post office. By the searching expression on his face, he might have been contemplating the best point of entry.

The building's frame creaked, leaned, and snapped as the roof caved in. The entire structure collapsed backward with a furious roar, as though a million voices had shouted agreement at once.

A stream of fire propelled higher into the sky. A gush of expelled flames followed by torrents of sparks and smoke.

In the house beside the one that was burning, a figure ran out in a nightdress. The figure was choking, holding its throat.

The older soldier walked toward it, and fired while he was walking.

The figure fell over.

The older soldier stood over the body, and stared to make certain.

He looked at the soldier with the tank on his back. "Refill your tank," he said, pointing toward the flames.

"One tank per fire, sir," the balding officer reminded him. "Due to the drought."

One side of the street had been entirely burned, a charred skeleton that continued to smoulder. The other side of the street was intact.

Above it all, the sky was splayed grey and black. The smell of soot lingered as the taste in everyone's mouths.

They set up a new office in the bakery. This was where the woman who had given him the bagels worked preparing dough. Four women in head scarves with flour on their noses and cheeks toiled in silence in the open bakery behind the counter.

The soldiers had salvaged a number of desks from the schoolhouse before it burned. There was furniture in the road. Bureaus and tables. Nothing of true value, as all articles deemed of worth had already been confiscated and forwarded to the regional treasury.

The filing cabinets in the town hall office could not be rescued, but the ones from the schoolhouse had been removed. Within the cabinets, there were files on all the residents as children. Obviously, these files had been overlooked.

The balding officer was encouraged by the discovery of the school files. He sat at his desk in the bakery, and hurried through each folder, anxious to reclaim an overview. It would not be too much of a chore to bridge the years between childhood and adulthood. In fact, the balding officer went at it as though it were an entertaining challenge. He would study a photograph and, soon, nodding, smile to himself, for he had exterminated many of the people in the files, and took pleasure in growing familiar with their young faces.

While the balding officer was busy writing on paper and updating files, an empty filing cabinet was brought in and set down beside the commander's desk.

He had not slept last night, his body mindful that it should be active in darkness. He sat behind his desk, and watched the balding officer, who occasionally glanced up at him with a relieved, conspiratorial expression.

The woman who had given him the bagels would peek at him when one of the other women broke down in tears and quietly wept.

He found his eyes drawn toward the woman.

The balding officer ignored all of it. Some time later, he rose and set down a number of papers on the commander's desk.

"Here," said the balding officer in an instructive tone, while pointing. "And there."

He signed each paper with the name they had called him.

The balding officer scrutinized the signatures, tapped the papers together in a neat stack, then went about arranging the freshly authorized documents in the filing cabinet.

From his desk, he had a clear view through the window.

A truck pulled up while he was wondering what he might do next. Whenever a vehicle arrived, he felt an inherent fear that his true identity had been discovered, and the transport was coming specifically for him.

He watched the driver walk toward the back of the truck, and raise the canvas flap to expose the emptiness within.

The driver came into the office. He was wearing a small cap on the top of his head.

Not needing instruction, the four women went about loading the truck with metal trays of baked goods.

"What happened there?" the driver asked the balding officer, glancing over his shoulder.

A stronger whiff of soot had trailed in after him.

"Insurgents," said the balding officer, still writing. "What does it matter to you? It's their own town."

The driver looked at him and said nothing.

He nodded.

When the women had finished loading the truck, the driver left the bakery and drove away.

None of this was new to either one of them.

CHAPTER 3

He assumed that the balding officer knew where he was going. The sedan continued bumping down the lone dirt road that had taken them out of town over a half hour ago.

Ahead of them, toward where the straight road stretched, there was nothing to hold their attention, save for the occasional mound of black remains.

"Let's hope they have a spare telewire," said the balding officer from the driver's seat. "Otherwise, our orders will have to arrive by transport. Delays lead to confusion. At this stage of the conflict, that could prove disastrous."

He nodded and made a noise, thinking of the burning woman, her knees, palms and forehead pressed against the floor. For reasons unknown to him, he thought that she might have been sent to him, that she had been his, and, now, she was lost. He could not remember her face. It had been ablaze when he first set eyes on her.

What am I doing, he wondered. What?

In a short while, they passed a number of military trucks pulled over on the side of the road. Seven soldiers were standing in the distance, facing the remnants of an old wall, as though studying it with vigilance.

What might be of such interest to them in rubble?

A few of the soldiers raised their hands to touch the wall

in the style of the condemned awaiting execution, but there was no firing squad at hand.

He turned his head to look at the balding officer, who was talking about one of the women in the bakery.

"The woman who gave you the bagels." Top lip pulled back, teeth pressed together. "I heard of that."

"What about her?" The tone he used gave the balding officer cause for hesitation.

The officer took a moment to check the road, while their proximity to one another became more pronounced.

He watched the officer's hand on the wheel.

"If I might ask a question of the commander."

"Yes?"

"What was the purpose of sending her back?"

"Back?"

"From Relief Camp 7." The balding officer glanced at him, as though a truth might be uncovered, or not.

Back from Relief Camp 7.

What he thought he knew of the woman vanished, and he was left trying to place her.

"We sent her out on transport, and you sent her back. It was unexpected."

"What do you mean?" He thought of the dead woman on the bed, her hair snipped erratically short. Was that who the woman reminded him of? He could make no sense of the similarity.

"They never come back."

One thought hooked in another, until there was a tangle.

The officer shifted his eyes toward the windshield, and nodded his head. "Here we are."

Up ahead, there was a town, much like the one they had left behind.

The sedan entered the street and the women – all naked and filthy – slowed to watch them roll by, their expressions flat, clay-tight, as though dug up and excused.

The balding officer introduced the commander by name, while the new officer stood from behind his desk in the post office to salute.

The new officer and the balding officer seemed familiar with each other. They exchanged glances. The balding officer nodded in a clandestine manner, as though there was a secret held between them, as though they might be old friends or brothers. One was much like the other, in appearance as well as vocal range.

The balding officer eyed the telewire, went to it, and quietly, gingerly touched its glass and metal top.

"We need to send a message, our telewire was lost. We require another."

"Certainly," said the new officer, his tone lacking civility to the point of disrespect. "By fire. Your files as well, I hear."

The balding officer looked at the new officer as though in challenge, but the new officer gave him no notice.

"The fire was set by insurgents," said the new officer, as though they might not have known this crucial bit of information. He settled back in his chair, and kept his hands on the armrests.

"They were dealt with," said the balding officer. "No further worries there."

"Aw." The new officer shifted his eyes from the balding officer to the commander. It seemed in his nature to be relentlessly curious. "I've heard quite a bit about you, commander."

He nodded.

"Might I ask you a question, sir?"

"Yes."

"As you know, I spent some time at Relief Camp 7. I was there shortly before your arrival."

"Oh?"

From the tone of the discourse, the balding officer appeared to be taking special notice.

"There was a man there." The new officer gave the man's name. "You know him, of course."

"Of course."

"In fact, it was you, personally, who ordered his invalidation."

He said nothing in reply, merely gave the new officer a look that might cause him to give particular consideration to the forthcoming selection of words.

"Your half-brother."

"Yes, I know." His eyes shifted to the balding officer, who was expressing supreme interest.

"I can't recall if it was by another mother or father."

"Mother," he blurted out, about to add a remark that might twin as a warning.

"Yes, of course." The new officer cut in. "One was of our faith, the other not. The mothers."

"Yes," raising his voice. "And your point?"

"Just to let you know, sir, that your orders were followed." He gave a slight nod of his head. "I handled it personally, on your behalf."

"Good."

"The resemblance is uncanny." The new officer glanced him up and down.

He checked the balding officer, and determined that

action was required. "Stand up," he said, flashing his eyes back on the new officer.

The comfortable and knowing look of penetration that had prided the new officer's expression faded at once. He pressed his hands against the armrests and stood up.

"Are you familiar with the word 'insubordination'?"

"Of course, sir."

"In word as well as in deed?"

"Yes, sir."

He drew his revolver from his holster, and levelled it at the new officer's face, while taking two steps around the desk. He pressed the hard point of the pistol to the officer's temple.

The new officer's eyes tried not to look at him. They strained to stare ahead.

A moment later, he turned the gun on the balding officer, then, deliberately, back on the new officer, aiming near the left eye, the eyelash blinking, fluttering against steel.

"Which one of you should die for this?"

The balding officer squinted, as did the new officer. They watched each other, as though wordlessly plotting to halt their disintegration.

"You think I'm stupid," he shouted, licking spittle from his bottom lip.

They shook their heads in unison.

In unison, he thought, then barked: "Kneel."

The new officer held up his hands, placed them on his head, and knelt.

"You," he said, pointing at the balding officer, who could not hide his open-mouthed astonishment, yet knelt regardless, in the same pose. "Over there."

The new officer walked on his knees toward the balding officer. Side by side, they were of the same rank. They wore the same uniform. The same boots. The same pins and insignias. They had the same face, one with a little more hair on his head than the other, but he could not tell which one. The one on the right? The one on the left?

"I'll ask you a question."

Neither of the two responded.

"Which one of you is unlike the other?"

They thought for only a moment, almost hopefully, before they were profoundly confused.

He repeated the question, spacing the words: "Which… one… of… you… is… unlike… the… other?"

He expected a show of hands. Still, there was no reply. He tried the question in another language, a language that flew out of him, and seemed composed for the timbre of that exact question.

He shouted at the top of his lungs, his voice booming hoarse: "Which one of you is unlike the other?" His index finger was sweaty and curled against the trigger. It wanted to tug the tension away, to charge the chaos out from his heart, down the length of his arm, to thicken his muscles with release, to inflict.

Yet neither one of them would raise their hand. They were trembling, their elbows shivering where they were angled out in the air.

He screamed and paced around the two men, until his face was a swell of red heat, and the men were sweating through a snivelling concert of tears.

"Brother," one of them whimpered at him. "Please."

He was struck still. "What?"

"We are brothers," said one through the snot. "The chosen ones."

The other piped up: "We are all brothers in this."

As though made impotent, he lowered the revolver.

"Brother," said one.

"Brother," said the other. Weeping with relief, he rocked back and forth, first placing his hands on his chest, then in front of his face, palms out. Bobbing, the officer began muttering words.

He holstered his revolver, then drew it again, and

fired at the one who had begun praying.

The prayer continued, barely changed, yet the eyes did, and the body, still on its knees, tilted slightly to the side, and fell backwards.

There was only one of them remaining. The balding officer, perhaps, or the new officer. It was a mystery to him now.

Although he was made anxious by the shooting, he had no way of knowing if what he had done was done correctly.

There were now two empty cartridges in the chambers of his revolver. The idea brought on a tremble in his arm that spread toward his shoulder, and then ticked into his cheek.

The only thing he seemed certain of was that the man on the floor was meant to die.

"Take the telewire," he said, holstering his revolver.

The remaining officer scrambled to his feet and – stepping over the body – made his way to the telewire, where he began disassembling the wires and the thin roll of paper on a spool.

Outside, the street was deserted. No doubt, they had heard his shouting from the post office. And, more notably, the percussion of the single gunshot.

While the remaining officer brought the disassembled telewire out of the post office, and loaded it into the sedan, the commander walked down the length of the street, calling out an order for evacuation to the houses on one side, then the other.

It seemed it might now be possible to save something from this place.

Women appeared in each doorway. They were naked. Knowing what must be done, they hurriedly formed a straight line across the width of the dirt road and turned away. Their backs to him, they bowed down on all fours, their foreheads to the earth.

The remaining officer shut the sedan trunk, and hurried over to the commander's side.

"Where are their clothes?" the commander asked the remaining officer, his heart thudding again.

"Confiscated to prevent escape." There was a sheen of sweat on the remaining officer's face, which now held a nervous expression that imparted his urgency to please. "A new order from just yesterday."

Two soldiers – a young one and an older one – walked up and down in front of the women, checking that their heads were bowed, their eyes to the dirt.

From the same father, he thought. Different mothers.

This was not his town. It was like his town, but it was not. He recognized not one of the women, old or young. They reminded him of no one.

He recalled shooting the officer in the post office. The bullet had entered the officer's mouth. The body was still there, on the floor, hidden behind walls. It might be dragged out and thrown down before these women, so they might see what he had done for them.

He watched the naked women in the street. It was all beginning to make sense.

From different mothers, he thought, yet he had no memory of who. No confusion came from this. It was not troubling. In fact, this sense of lacking was almost pleasing to him; the way he felt prompted the statement: "Show me what happens next."

The remaining officer gave him a buoyant look, as though the commander might be coming to his senses.

"Selfsameness procedure?" asked the remaining officer, already drawing his nightstick.

The commander nodded.

It was a relief to the remaining officer. His step held the tempered agility of a sprint, as he went from one woman to the next with exceptional vigour, bending forward and thrusting his arm back and forth while sounds were roused from the women.

The women bore the remaining officer's willingness as best they could. They endured. They did not complain. Not one of them. In this way, they were invariable.

It was no secret that the remaining officer was pleased to be back in command of his little patch.

The younger and older soldiers stood to each side of the woman the remaining officer was breaching, should an attempt at withdrawal require quashing.

One of the soldiers spat and called a woman, "unclean dog."

When the remaining officer had finished with the line, he returned to the commander's side. His night stick glistened with fluid of a colour that could not be determined because of its hard blackness.

"Back into your houses now," the commander said, almost pitying them.

The women fanned out before him. A few were hobbling, while others walked slowly or in haste.

Any one of them, he thought, studying their bodies.

A different mother.

It was peculiar the way they moved off, at uneven paces, some wishing to conceal their nudity, others not bothered by it.

His attention was held by an older, grey-haired woman, the way her buttocks were loose, her heavy breasts stretched and hanging, her stomach slack and wrinkled scar-like, the way her step was impeded by some arthritic ailment as she hobbled away, her eyes on her feet. She clutched at the plain wooden railing as she went up onto her step.

It was a chore to watch her.

Once the old woman had entered her house, the commander followed after her.

She was standing by a lone wooden chair in her living room when he entered. There were no artefacts hung on the walls. Above the small, makeshift stove, the shelf displayed nothing, not even dust.

He watched the old woman's face; her eyes were cast down so that he might not connect with her, her arms hung from sloped shoulders at her sides.

He walked around the empty room, his boots sounding against the swept floorboards. Pacing felt natural to him.

This is not my town, he thought.

He felt his breath turn hotter in his nostrils as he explored the space that had been cleared of everything. He shot a glance back at the old woman.

Whose mother?

He paused to search out the window. A group of four men in uniforms were gathered in an unruly circle, engaged in discussion. He thought he might shoot a few of them for sport.

One of the soldiers looked toward the doorway of the house.

As the commander trod nearer the window, his boot disturbed a loose floorboard, and his step faltered. He looked down to hear the old woman whimper.

The old woman was using her eyes on him now. They were meant to change him, distract him, dissuade him.

He bent to straighten the floorboard, and caught a glimmer of golden light beneath it. Kneeling, he shifted the floorboard away to discover a small frame bordering a photograph of a man in a robe from a period he did not recognize.

The old woman ran toward him, her bare soles slapping the floorboards. Already she was screeching and snatching for the photograph.

"No," she cried, clamping her bony, wrinkled fingers onto the frame, and yanking with surprising muscle.

He released his hold, allowed her to have it, for it meant something honourable to her.

The old woman clutched the photograph in both

hands. As she stared down at it, tears filled her brown eyes, and a blush – a stain of concealed blood – infused her grey face with life.

The commander explored the hole with his fingers, stretching his arm deeper into the chasm, until he felt something like hair that edged away from him, the strand slipping through his fingertips. At first, he suspected vermin, yet the length and the curl of the hair bettered his belief.

Bending his face to the hole, he searched down and over.

The old woman was making noises that forewarned him of inevitable hysteria.

He looked up and put a finger to his lips.

She slapped her hand over her mouth, and wept, hugging the frame to her bare bosom, and whimpering behind her palm.

Again, he lowered his eyes to the hole, tilted his head, to prevent blocking the light, so that wedges of light might reveal what was hidden beneath the house.

He heard child-like whispering, then stillness.

"Here," he said.

The old woman nearly cried out.

"Come here," he said into the hole. He waited, but

nothing happened. "I won't harm you."

Again, the old woman fussed.

He looked at her.

She was shaking her head. Panicky, she gazed toward the window, and removed her hand from her mouth to point.

The soldiers had drifted nearer, as though to see what might be proceeding inside, where proof of the legendary status of the commander might be witnessed and stand as testimony.

"It's just me," the old woman muttered consolingly to him. "Me… me…"

The commander searched back into the hole, and saw the white of an eye, the slimly lit arc of a young face, the curl of black hair.

A girl.

He smiled for what seemed like treasonous reasons.

"How do you get down there?" he asked the old woman.

She shook her head. Fretfully, she checked toward the window, and tapped her heart with her fist.

"Tell me. I'm not who you think I am." He watched her naked body, the meaty thickness of her breasts and hips, the unruly tangle of her pubis, and thought he might give up on this, might do what he suspected he came here to do. But then there was the thought of the young eye beneath the floorboards, the photograph in the old woman's arms, the house she had built around herself.

He reached down into the hole, scouting around, until he felt something wooden, bobbing near his fingers. He took hold of it, brought it halfway up through the hole, but had to turn it sideways to fit it fully through. It was a clock. The time, perhaps, correct.

He reached down and there were other items at his fingertips, as though they were being handed to him at once to avoid the grasp of something dearer.

A gold, embroidered scarf.

A small book in which poems were handwritten in deep-green ink.

A white robe which the old woman grabbed up and slapped against her body, as though in deliverance.

"How do you get under here?" he asked.

Boot steps on the front landing.

The commander stared at the old woman, almost recognizing her now; that robe she held against her body so becoming.

The front door opened, and the remaining officer stepped in, his stride charged with significance.

The old woman shuffled back, pressing the robe tighter against her skin.

From his holster, the remaining officer drew his revolver, and aimed it at the old woman, who knelt and dropped the robe, but retained her one-handed grip on the frame which she clenched upright against the top of her head. Her other open palm pressed at the air, as though to hold back the moment. Trembling, she lowered the frame, and held it over her face with both hands.

The remaining officer shot the old woman in the head, shattering the glass.

The old woman spun in a graceful curve, and fell over on her side. The frame hit the floor, its bottom corner sticking into the wood like a knife, while bits of glass tinkled around her.

"Sir?" said the remaining officer, only now seeing the commander still on his knees.

The commander covered the hole with the board. "A hiding place for trinkets," he said, more interested in the old woman, who groaned and twisted, until she was motionless on her belly.

Fluid crept in a living pool away from her head.

On her belly, her legs and arms apart, her head turned away, the old woman would never set eyes on him again.

"Leave us alone," he said.

The remaining officer holstered his revolver, gave one nod, and backed away.

The front door was shut.

The commander rose from his knees, and went toward the old woman, until he was standing over her. He then shifted nearer. With the tip of his boot, he nudged her tattooed foot. The dirty heel tilted one way.

In this position, so near the dead, he felt himself come to life.

From beyond the window, the raucous laughter of men.

CHAPTER 4

The drive back was travelled in silence. He held the image of that town in his head, until he entered his own, and the memory was replaced.

The remaining officer was the first out of the car.

The commander sat in the passenger seat, and watched through the window.

Across the street, women were still picking through the charred rubble.

The remaining officer hurriedly spoke to the two soldiers, who listened and nodded, looked where the remaining officer was pointing from house to house along the unburned side of the street, then to the women poking through the remnants of their belongings.

He would not remove himself from the sedan nor roll down the window to clearly hear what instructions were being dispatched.

Then the two soldiers promptly strode away, accosted the women, and tore off their garments.

The women clutched at themselves and wailed.

He found comfort in the sensation of being sealed inside, while he watched the soldiers hurry off to enter doorways, and come out some time later with shreds of clothing – held away from themselves as though soiled – which they piled in the centre of the road.

When all of the houses had been entered and the new orders carried out, gasoline was chucked onto the mound of clothes and set afire.

The flames burned as the coloured tears of clothing that lay along the periphery were held up by sticks and dropped in.

The remaining officer stood beside the two soldiers, and slapped the younger one on the back. The way his mouth was moving, the remaining officer seemed to be conveying a comical story that had been imported from another place to here.

The commander wondered what new part of him might now exist with these three others.

There had been no dreams. No sleep since his journey from the pile of bodies. But when his eyes finally shut that night, his head was crowded.

When he awoke in the morning, calmed by a good night's rest, he sorted through the images that remained audibly and visually dear to him.

The female faces veiled by smoke.

The stir of lips muttering for forgiveness.

The horizon obliterated by black dots of supplicated bodies, knelt in submission, knelt in pious surrender.

Already, his room above the bakery was filled with the warm scent of baking that led him to believe it might be another day. Sunlight was sunlight, after all. It was there through the glass in his bedroom window.

He heard the voice of the remaining officer barking beneath him. He rose and dressed.

First, he brushed his hair with the silver brush, and then he combed it. His hair would need to be trimmed soon if he were to conform to regulations.

Standing before the mirror, it was impossible not to catch glimpses of his face in reflection. Where his eyes had not interested him in the slightest, had not seemed to involve him, nor invoke him, they now became more fascinating by the moment.

He stared into them, until he felt himself drawn to his likeness.

The remaining officer was standing near the corner, muttering about the diabolical threat of technology, while attempting to connect the telewire to current.

Having come from his upstairs room through the doorway above the alley and climbed down the outside wooden stairs, the commander now stood at the front of the shop.

The remaining officer noticed the commander after a few moments and – red faced – straightened to snap out a salute.

The commander saw that there were only two women working in the bakery now. They were both naked, save for their head scarves, which they had been permitted to don to prevent hair from falling into their baked goods.

He recalled the old woman who had been shot, and the young face whispering secretively beneath the floorboards. Back in that town, when he had finished with the duties required of him, as attached to the old woman, he had uncovered the loose floorboards once again and searched down there. Obtaining a crowbar from one of the soldiers, he had worked to tear up a section of floorboards. The space was wide enough for him to drop into.

Hunched in the gap and crawling amid the dirt, he had found only a pile of earth-encrusted bones toward the far corner. There was no young girl. This had angered him, for he had plans to save the girl, in his own singular way.

The woman who had given him the two bagels would not meet his eyes. She went about her work, trying not to be ashamed. Her body was well-made, natural, despite the markings.

The other woman was larger and laboured with crude

energy, as though the absence of clothing held no bearing over her. She was an obstinate worker.

The commander stepped deeper into the room and neared his desk. He touched the back of his chair, and thought of sitting. If he took his place behind the desk, he would have to appear to be engaged in duties.

The remaining officer gave the commander the occasional bit of obligatory attention, while continuing with his responsibilities.

In a number of minutes, the telewire made a noise resembling the discharge of a minuscule machine gun, and began printing off a narrow strip of paper.

The remaining officer made a sound of delight, and stood smiling over the paper, reading along as it inched out, his eyes eager for directives. When the printing was completed, he tore off the paper, and brought it to the commander.

Still standing by his desk, the commander read the words.

As the enemy was making headway within once-secured borders, it was required that all female prisoners be transported at the earliest possible convenience.

The remaining officer gave immediate attention to the two women at work.

The commander looked toward the two women, until the two women stopped working to regard the commander and the remaining officer.

"Who will cook for us?" asked the remaining officer.

"The retention of essential workers has been authorized," the commander answered. "Here." He laid a finger against the words on the paper. "One per officer. Assigned as required and approved by the district commander."

The remaining officer went to the heavier woman in the bakery, as though she were another chore that needed dealing with. Gruffly, he clutched her by the arm.

The heavier woman's hands were white with flour. She wiped them on the sides of her thick legs as she was jostled toward the back door.

"You're lucky today," said the remaining officer as he hurried her out. "You've been approved." With this, he slapped her right buttock, and flashed his teeth at the commander.

The black-haired woman looked at him. The front of her body was a catastrophe of injuries. She turned away, exposing the length of her back, which was beautifully untouched. Not a mark. The commander studied her shoulder muscles moving as she shaped the dough with her hands.

He was stepping toward her without thought. The nearer he came, the more peculiar he felt. So close. He stood behind her, marvelling at the texture of her skin. She knew that he was there, yet she would not turn.

"Look at me," he said, less of an order, more of a commiserating request.

The woman stopped doing her work, and slowly faced him, her gaze lowered to the ground.

This one younger, he said to himself. Lovely in a way that cooled his temper.

"Please, look at me." He set his finger under her chin, and raised her head, tipping her brown eyes to his.

He thought that he might tell her about how he had come from the pile of bodies, how he knew that that was wrong of him to do. That he was at fault, yet he did not know why.

He had no idea why he was once in the pile of bodies, and now here, able to put people in the pile of bodies. How was that possible? he wanted to ask her. She might have an answer. Or she might be one of them. Dead. His bidding.

He realized that his jaw and eyes were set with an expression of blankness. It would be impossible for her to tell anything from him.

Again, she lowered her eyes, because what she was

seeing did nothing to convince her, to hold her to him.

"I have no idea who I am," he said in a choked voice.

She raised her eyes to see him this time. So full of consideration.

After a moment, she said in a pure-hearted voice, "I know who you are."

The younger soldier was removing a cloth that had been tied around the bottom half of his face. He had taken off his jacket, and set down his rifle. His hands were stained. He rubbed at them, brought them toward his nostrils, but stopped himself. The expression on his face indicated distaste. A human admission.

When he noticed the commander, he saluted and said, "The bodies have been delivered, sir."

The older soldier came up behind the younger one. He stepped with fluidity and menace, like something fearless on the prowl. He was not wearing a mask to protect him from the stench. More than a single bullet would be required to bring him down.

"You wanted them in the houses, sir?" asked the younger soldier.

"They will fill the houses," said the older soldier confidently, rubbing away a spot on his palm with his thumb, his concentration entirely inward.

"Where are they now?"

The younger soldier pointed down the alleyway from where they had just come. "Behind there at the back. Outside, for now."

He walked into the alleyway, treading the length of the buildings, until gaining sight of the pile of bodies.

Faltering, he remembered, yet what he pictured was not the same. Memory, detached from presence by a disjoining inner lurch, spirited him away.

The pile was not as large as the image held in mind, not stacked so high, but spread out over a greater area. It troubled him, for the sight – one of his single memories deemed true – did not fit with recollection, and so he was rattled, as though a tremor had gone off.

The bodies were not grey, but tinted pink. The colour not to be trusted.

He quickly turned to challenge the two soldiers coming up behind him. "Where did you get these?" he demanded.

"Relief Camp 7, sir," the younger soldier assured him.

He strode nearer to the tangle of bodies.

There were no flies, no signs of illness, decomposition or harm. The bodies appeared to be at rest, their eyes shut in repose, as though they might stir through a series of awakenings at any moment.

"What?" he asked, incredulously, but he did not want an answer, for to believe in the answer would mean going out of his head. "When did you get these?"

"Today."

"These aren't the bodies," he shouted from a prod of fear. "Where?"

"Relief Camp 7, sir," the younger soldier maintained.

The older soldier watched the commander, as though it might be some sort of trick. He laughed once, then, thinking better of it, frowned toward greater focus.

"I came from the bodies," the commander said. "I was there. These are not the bodies." He stared back at the jumble, expecting a different view. "These are," his eyes scanned to rest here and there, "fresher."

"These are the bodies that were there, sir," said the older soldier in a disbelieving tone that approached rebuke.

He thought of the two officers on their knees, back in the town that was like this town, yet not his own. At once, he walked toward the older soldier and gave a shove. The contact jolted his arms.

Taken by surprise, the older soldier stumbled back, almost tripped, yet regained his footing.

The second shove knocked him down, his hands

at his sides to brace the earth.

The older soldier was scared, yet somehow made meaner by his fright.

The commander drew his revolver and fired into the older soldier's chest – where he supposed the heart had grown – fired until the chambers were filled with empty shells.

He could not stop his hot breath from raging. It was magnificent and crippling, paralyzing in a way that made him peerless. Thinking to complete the chore, he whipped his head around to confront the younger soldier.

"Where are the bodies?" he shouted, striding toward the younger soldier, who backed away and held up his palms in defensive uncertainty. "Where?"

"These..."

"Kneel," he shouted.

The younger soldier knelt. "Please." He joined his hands to his chest in prayer.

The commander levelled the revolver, "Where?" With his free arm, he drew his sleeve across his mouth. "Where?" Jabbing his empty revolver forward. "Where? Where?"

"These," begged the younger soldier, loosely pointing toward the bodies, while staring up. "These were there, sir. These are the bodies, I swear."

The commander stopped and scanned the corpses, then darted a look at the dead, older soldier. He holstered his revolver, marched to the older soldier, and bending down, unbuttoned the soldier's shirt, pulled off his boots, his pants…

Grabbing the naked soldier's foot, the commander dragged the body toward the pile.

"Come here," he demanded.

The younger soldier rose from his knees, and obediently took hold of the naked soldier's arm.

"Lift… and…"

They swung the naked soldier, back and forth, and then – on the commander's word – they released.

The body landed with a fleshy thud.

The commander breathed deeply, watching as grey veins skulked outward through the pile.

"You see," the commander said, again wiping spittle from his chin.

Grey and green, the bodies stared, each one of them with their limbs slowly bending and twisting in a rippling creak of sounds, until they attained the physical crook of ones haphazardly disposed of.

"These are the ones." Gladdened, the commander thrust his index finger in the air, his breath burning in his lungs. "These, you see, these ones..."

The younger soldier gazed up at the sky as a black cloud of flies descended like the battering of a storm.

There was a knock on his door while he rested in bed.

"Yes," he said, pulling his mind away from going over the day's events that were remarkably vivid, yet barred from the stillness of his room.

The door eased open, and the black-haired woman from the bakery was standing there, peering in. She entered the room on bare feet, the scarf no longer on her head. Nude, she paused a moment, perhaps awaiting instruction. Then – as though recalling the proper conduct and procedure – she shut the door.

Only one side of the woman's body was revealed in the dim light that cast its diagonal bar through the window.

The commander watched her legs, then higher, not knowing what might be the appropriate play at action. How well had this woman known the man he had shot at Relief Camp 7?

His hands were joined behind his head, his fingers meshed. It was a strain to look at her this way, so he turned on his side.

Once he had settled, he heard the woman swallow. It

was enough to watch her in this light, yet he felt a need to relieve the woman of some of her expectation. He tried thinking of words, and the words he thought of glazed his eyes.

In the woman's presence, the commander felt hopeless, helpless.

Should he pat the bed beside him? Should he give her explicit instruction? Should he wait for her to offer the first greeting?

From beyond the window, there came the far-off sound of a bomb discharging.

In a quiet voice, the woman said: "It's like you don't remember me."

His eyes mindfully went over her face to see how the swelling in his heart changed his view of it.

"You saved me," she said.

"No."

"You did. I am yours."

"Mine?"

"Yes."

"By heart or by chain?"

She smiled a little, knowing there was no harm intended. "Both… because you saved me." But her smile lasted only moments before she, once again, became moderate.

"You can go away if you like," he said, not meaning the words, wanting to add: I would prefer you remained. His eyes tried not to trace the artful lines of her body, how they were interrupted by the welts and scars.

"Do you want me to stay?"

He nodded.

The woman stepped toward the bed, and sat on the edge of it with her back to him. Her right palm rested against the mattress.

He studied her back, now fully in the light, the nubs of her spine. The design of her was something to behold. He wanted to touch there, yet the gesture would place him above her.

After a minute, the woman lay back, drew in her legs and straightened her body beside his. She remained still and watched the ceiling.

His eyes skimmed over her body.

With the woman this near, the commander could not help but recall the photographs of her tucked away in the file that had burned. The memory of the open wounds excited him, yet the sight of the scars softened him.

That was action, he thought.

Excitation.

This is eventuality.

The scars. Longevity. What must be lived with.

The sight of her profile made him lean forward to kiss her cheek.

She turned her face to look at him, her eyes brown, her lips full.

She was wondering about him, about men.

He skimmed his hand along her shoulder, down the smooth length of her arm.

"I've heard what you've done to people. Why not to me?"

He gave a short shake of his head, his left wrist beginning to deaden with his hand propping up his head that way. "Not me." He eased down, so that his eyes were in line with hers.

"Was it because you were in love with me?"

He sighed through his nostrils. "I don't know."

A moment of silence before she said: "If only they could eat up the shame of being a whore to everyone."

The sound of "whore" prickled under his skin. It spurred the boldness, the bravery required to slip his fingertips over her breast, toward the centre, where he circled her nipple.

"I don't want to catch this," she said, her eyes dipping

toward his groin, where she felt him stiffening against the side of her leg.

"Catch what?"

"Catch any more of this." Her eyes went to the ceiling, then to the window.

Her caution made him smile.

"What I'll catch from you," she continued, her eyes finding his again. "Any more of this outbreak."

He kissed her lips.

As his lips left hers, she whispered, "That's why I'm just your whore, for the preservation of deeper feeling. Is that why you saved me?"

"For the preservation of deeper feeling."

"No, because I am your whore."

"Are you?"

"Yes."

"Not by heart then, by chain."

When he had done to her what was expected, he tried rising off of her body, but she clutched onto him, one palm pressed warmly against his back, one arm tightening behind his neck.

"Don't you dare move," she said, having just reached climax.

He lifted his head from the feel and smell of her hair to look at her face.

I helped you the second time, he thought, in the alleyway. But I killed the man who helped you first.

Tear trails shone at the corners of her eyes towards her temples, while she watched him.

In her stare, he had the feeling that it was not him she was watching.

He kissed her warm, moist lips, in a shot at evasion. The emotion given in return compelled him to kiss her again, with his tongue and with his right hand coming up to caress her cheek.

"Why are you so calm?" she asked. "You were never so calm before."

He lay on his side and stared at her face. She was watching the ceiling, her arms straight at her sides.

A moment later, he lay on his back, so that both of them were fixed in the same pose, studying the ceiling.

At that point, he turned his head to regard the door, expecting it to open. A curious man stepping in, raising a revolver to unleash ruin.

He glanced at the woman's profile, and the confusion buckled in his chest. Every frailty of sentiment seemed to have been blanched from the room.

"Why are you here?" he asked, confused now, almost cross.

"Because you saved me."

"No." He sighed and turned his head toward the ceiling. How could he go about asking her these questions without revealing the deficiency of who he was?

Again, he turned his head to regard her.

Her hands were joined on her scarred belly, tattooed fingers meshed, opened eyes so reasonably clear.

He could not understand why. He waited for her to blink. It took a while. "What are you to me? I need to know."

"I don't know," she said. "That's your decision."

"Why am I here? We here?"

"I don't know."

"You don't understand." Urgently, he rose up on one elbow.

Her eyes became frightened at once, as though she might have been expecting this, her hands pressed into her belly, yet she continued staring above.

"I am here because I am less than you," she said. It was the thing to say, an oath relevant to the times. "Unclean. Your untouchable whore."

"But I came from the bodies."

"I know that you make the bodies. I might have been one of them, but you—"

"No, no, no." There was a tightness in his head and shoulders that made him want to slap her for misunderstanding. "I came from the pile of bodies, from inside, under."

The black-haired woman turned her head to see him with new eyes that had been kept private up to that point. She shifted a little; her muscles and skin seemed at ease. Her breath, sweetened, moved with greater affinity. "What do you mean?" she asked with secretive pleasure.

"I crawled out from the centre." He waited a stretch of time for his words to sink toward their mark. "I was supposed to be dead."

"Why?" Her eyes flicked over his features. "But you're just like him."

Perhaps she was too interested now. Suddenly, with dread, he intuited that her concern might gouge a trail to the end of him.

"Am I?" he said vaguely.

"Why are you telling me this? To trick me?"

"No."

She regarded his eyes, then his forehead and chin.

"I am the enemy," he said, the words slipping out.

"Yes," she said.

"No." The commander gently shook his head. "Not your enemy."

"I know what you mean."

"I can't remember." He stared at her, at once feeling that his need for her had inexplicably grown innate. "It was my brother. That's what I think."

"How can you know for certain?"

"I was with the dead. Why would I be with the dead?" And then, in a vacant tone, he went over the details of the story, from the climbing out, to the shooting of his twin, to the drive through the checkpoints, to the story from this town forward.

"But that man from the shed, the one who was on the bed with the woman, he is in the pile of bodies now."

"Yes."

"He looked like you?"

"Yes, very much." His eyes became expectant, as though the black-haired woman might know more of him than she had first let on.

"But you're in control now."

"Yes."

"Then how are you unlike him?"

CHAPTER 5

The voices of women in the dawn woke him. They spoke to one another in worried bits of words that shivered in through the gap in his slightly raised window.

Seeing that the woman from the bakery was no longer by his side, he stood up from the bed and went to the window, searching for her figure.

He was still unaccustomed to the mortification of the women's nakedness. He watched down into the street while he buttoned the front of his shirt.

Women had been gathered together by the younger soldier and remaining officer, and were being helped up into the truck. Only three were not loaded.

By the time he was done fastening his buttons, all of the women were safely stowed away.

He finished dressing, went down the side entrance, into the alleyway, then out into the street.

Already, the sun was a blaze in the sky.

He squinted and turned his back to it.

"There's one old woman," the younger soldier anxiously notified him, pointing two houses up from the bakery, "who won't come out. Should I shoot her where she stands?"

The remaining officer looked him up and down,

while pulling tight the ropes that secured the flap at the back of the truck.

"Let me see," the commander said, and walked toward the house. On the way, he pulled on his new coat, straightened the collar, the raised star insignias felt by his thumbs.

There was no need to knock, the door had been removed from its hinges. A crescent moon, like the one he had seen in the sky his first night there, had been painted in green next to the open doorway.

His boots sounded along the hollow flooring as he stepped toward the old woman who stood cowering in the centre of the room.

There was nothing in the room, save for a wooden chair. All of the space had been swept clean.

"It's time for you to go," he said, as though taking up a conversation where it had been left off.

The old woman's arms dangled by her sides. She was naked. Sorry.

He looked down at her breasts, and noticed the wide nipples, the decrepitly erotic sag of her skin.

Not in this town, he told himself. My town.

He turned and stared at the floor near the window. Already, he could hear the whispers multiplying in his ears.

The hiding place had become obvious to him, yet the

voices seemed not to care, as though they assumed allegiance.

The whispering grew from a shush of warnings to the invariable noise of traitorous mutterings.

Sighing, he looked at the old woman.

What was his place in this house?

He was meant to be an intruder who claimed to belong. No, demanded to belong. Assumed. No, not to belong, but to own. Own this. Own her. Her obliteration.

In truth, his place in this house was to know nothing of it.

It was with reluctance that he turned and stepped toward the loose floorboards. Going down on his knees, he lifted the planks.

There was the picture frame, lying in the dirt. A man was featured in the photograph. He was wearing a uniform, and there was a teenaged girl standing by his side.

He took up the frame, recognizing the girl's face. It was the black-haired woman from the bakery. She belonged in this house, with this old woman. It was here that she belonged in a casual time when he might meet her, and treat her to a night at the cinema.

Peering down into the hole, he saw no movement. He leaned to reach deeper into the hollow to discover what might have been secreted away. He strained to search, sensing the warmth of something brushing up against his hand, followed by a piercing nip at his fingertip. So painful was the injury that he yanked back his hand, and savagely cursed on an intake of breath.

There was blood on the tip of the index finger of his left hand. The curve of the tip and an arc of the fingernail had been ripped loose. Clamped in a flinch of pain that he cringed through, he gingerly pressed the chunk of flesh back into place, meaning to seal the wound.

At once, he rose, hurling the frame away. It skimmed, then shimmied along the floorboards, the photograph facing up, toward the ceiling.

He held his finger together, while taking inventory of the damage done, the spill of warm blood along his palm, where it trickled at the edge.

He flashed his eyes at the hole, his face red with anger, his blood dripping into the hollow, to stain the dirt.

"What is down there?" he demanded of the old woman, yanking a handkerchief from his back pocket, and binding it around his hand.

"Nothing," she said.

"There is something," he assured her, pulling the knotted handkerchief tighter with his teeth.

"No," she said, calmly, reasonably. "Nothing. Nothing is there."

"Look." He held up his hand, the handkerchief stained with fresh blood. "Look." With his right hand, he drew his empty revolver and aimed it toward the hole.

"No," the old woman shouted with fright.

"No?"

"No," she said, calmly this time. "Nothing. Please," calmer still, "there is nothing."

"Nothing? This done by nothing?"

With assured eyes that delved into his, eyes that understood and recognized, she paid attention in a doting way that aroused him through his rage. "Yes," she said, her voice soothing. "Nothing. Please. Shush, shush… it is nothing, my son."

"Nothing did this?" He could not help but chuckle, noticing how his other hand was now stained. Blood spreading from the wound. It was absurd. "You expect me to believe in that?" The pain came at him in a rush that was oddly electric.

The old woman's eyes shifted to the revolver. In them, there was the deepness of longing. "Please," she said, placing two fingertips to the space above her heart. "Please, this is where you catch what's hidden. What harmed your finger."

He laughed through the pain, "A heart with teeth."

"Buried."

He laughed again, this time inwardly, "A buried heart with teeth."

The old woman's eyes remained on the revolver, while he stepped toward her to set the barrel against the spot she had indicated.

He glanced back at the trail of his blood, leading from the hole to his boots, the wide smear of it too exaggerated for such a minor wound. Already, the trail was darkening from deep red to black.

The old woman lowered her eyes, watching the metal against her skin, the way the circle dented her grandmotherly flesh.

"Please," she said. "This is where it is all hidden, full to the point of bursting."

This close, he smelled the oldness of her. When he looked at her chest again, the barrel of the revolver was not pressed there, but his injured fingertip. The old woman had switched one for the other, her hand curled around the length of his finger.

"Who is ever grateful for the authority of touch?"

The pain in his fingertip throbbed like something rabid, desirous of its own will.

"What else was there left to do," she said, "but hide everything in the foundation?" Her eyes went to the hole in the floorboards that remained uncovered.

A few earth-encrusted artefacts, previously buried, were now protruding from the clay.

The sight of it set off an explosion.

It was not until the old woman had fired that he suspected she had taken possession of his revolver.

A wad of flesh struck the window across the room.

The glass in the picture frame crackled with a web of lines.

Heavy metal thunked to the floor.

He looked down to see a large exit wound through the woman's wrinkled and sagging chest, too great a hole for a single bullet.

The old woman's legs shuddered. Unable to support herself, she fell back against the chair, sat there and watched him.

The commander looked at his hand, the pain in his fingertip vanquished.

Why had he thought the chambers empty?

He turned his eyes to the revolver. By the looks of it, he believed that it might not be his. He bent and picked it up to find it cold.

"The worst weaponry," uttered the old woman, her eyes set on something beyond him, through the window toward the burnt buildings across the road, through the burnt buildings and through the sky. "They blame you," the old woman whispered hoarsely, "until you blame your own existence."

Selflessly, the old woman slipped away.

The commander noticed how the hole in her chest was filled with living things.

A screech sounded outside and advanced nearer. Through the door, a naked body rushed in, long black hair swept back, limbs and breasts swaying.

The younger soldier entered after her, in close pursuit.

The woman from the bakery saw the old woman's slumped body, and stumbled, her hands to her mouth. A hodgepodge of sound jittered from her: gasping, choking, weeping.

Crumbling to her knees, she clutched at the old woman, and uttered words mingled with a name. She stared at the gaping, ragged-edged hole, then fired a hate-filled look back at the commander.

"It was by her own hand," he said.

"Why… why would you say that," she cried, throwing

her arm toward the other soldiers in the room. "What they always say. It's not our own doing."

The younger soldier found this amusing. He smiled and shook his head with a glimmer of esteem in his eyes. He was watching the black-haired woman's backside where she was bent near the old woman.

You are growing up, the commander thought. Only so much more of this to make you a man with misgivings.

In a gesture of lewd frivolity, the younger soldier stomped forward and shoved the old woman from her chair.

The woman from the bakery scrambled to catch the body, cushioning it with her arms a moment before it struck the floor.

"We know who you are now," the younger soldier scoffed at the black-haired woman, his eyes set on the tangle of hair mounded out around her slitted centre. Again, he smiled, hopeful of encouragement, while exuding a whiff of rivalry, his nostrils flaring.

"Something dies," commented the younger soldier. "And something is left alone to manage."

The woman from the bakery wept and clutched at the old woman, until the younger soldier took hold of her arm, drawing her to her feet.

"You," she screamed at the commander. "You aren't

even one of them." She raged forward, struck him in the chest with a small, hard fist. "You are a liar." Her wet eyes glared above a snot-filled nose and buckled mouth. She poked his chest with such force that it hurt terribly, inciting him to grab hold of her wrist.

He watched her with what he suspected to be a look of warning.

From behind her, the old woman groaned, then farted.

The woman from the bakery broke away and threw herself down at the old woman. Wailing, she tilted her head to the old lips and fell silent, carefully listened, her eyes moving erratically, as though to catch the hobbling progression of an invisible spectacle.

The old woman remained still. There was no more life left in her.

"Awwww," screamed the black-haired woman, making fists above her head and rising, turning and pointing at him.

The younger soldier grabbed hold of her arm, turned it behind her back, then wrapped a length of her hair around his free hand, and pulled.

"He isn't even one of you," she said, struggling to yank away, oblivious to the pain in her arm, neck, and at the roots of her hair. "He told me so. He isn't one of you." Such torment needing to find voice. "He came from the bodies, from inside the pile of bodies. He's one of us, killing us now."

All of these words from an act of suicide.

"I could say the same about you," he countered, in defence of himself, learning, yet regretting at once.

"Should I put her in the truck?" asked the younger soldier.

He watched the woman's eyes. His decision. He remembered the woman in his bedroom last night. She was nothing like this woman now.

Already the old woman was being dragged from the room by the remaining officer.

"You," screamed the woman from the bakery, her teeth exposed, her frenzied expression gnarled by savagery. She tried to claw at his face, her fingernails urgently near his cheek, barely brushing his lips. "You murderous nobody."

The commander remained in the old woman's living room until the sound of the truck's engine shrank away.

He sat on the single wooden chair and stared at the opened floorboards, until there was tranquilizing silence.

Then he stood and began climbing the steps to the second storey.

Halfway up, the stairs took a sharp right turn, the second set bringing him in line with a hallway.

Immediately, there were opened doors on his right and left, both rooms empty. Bare floors. Bare walls. Curtainless window panes. Space enervated by the energy of people having moved on.

Further ahead, to his right, there was another empty room, and, at the very end of the hallway, facing him, a shut door.

He reached for the knob, fearing that it might be locked, that someone might have been hidden away in there.

The knob turned freely in his hand.

He pulled open the door to face a wall of articles, tightly packed from floor to ceiling. A storage room. Yet, according to the architecture of the house, the room must have been as large as either of the bedrooms.

Not another item could have been crammed into the space.

Reaching ahead, the commander took hold of the wooden handle of an empty suitcase that had been flatly slid in. He drew it free and laid it upright beside him. Then he gripped the silver base of a lamp. The shade dislodged and crumbled beneath the weight of objects pushing down from above. He let the base of the lamp drop to the floor, then tossed out a typewriter in a case, a tray of noisy utensils, a bag of buttons, a plump, yellow pillow with tassels...

He continued digging, reaching forward, deeper and deeper, bending at the waist, as the beginning of a tunnel was gradually cleared.

The commander leaned on his stomach and edged ahead, his feet rising from the floor. In this position, his breathing became close, while cold objects pressed upon all parts of his body.

A more comfortable position was achieved when he turned on his side.

Settled, he worked to pry loose and expel items, so that a greater width was created near his chest. He removed smaller pieces (a tin of body powder, several pairs of shoes, a child's medal) from around a phonograph, which he worked back and forth, until it was dislodged. He squeezed it down the front of his body, then used his feet to kick it out of the tunnel where it clunked onto the floor.

Pleased with himself, he went on a spree of flicking smaller articles back out through the hole.

As he wormed his way deeper, he navigated a turn to the left, discerning a hint of glowing red up ahead. He continued gripping and expelling articles until he could see – through a clutter of bound envelopes, a hat box and a stuffed lizard – a red blanket behind which, he assumed, was a window.

The red blanket had been pinned up to block or filter light.

Carefully, he cleared away an adding machine and a tin punched vase, then pulled at the blanket, but the surrounding items continued holding the fabric against the wall and window casing.

The only way through was to tear a hole in the centre. A small, moth-eaten hole had already been started. He pried his finger into it, and pulled, squinting as pure light spilled in.

He ripped the opening bigger, shredding a vertical line down the blanket, until a pane of glass was revealed. A window at the back of the house, which gave him a view of the pile of bodies that the older soldier had been tossed into.

The commander watched the pile of bodies, startled by the sight of movement.

This time, he knew better. He would not be deceived.

Yet, as he continued watching, he witnessed something substantial emerge from the top of the mound, something less eager to enter the pile as to be free of it.

A hand that grasped at open air.

Moments later, an entire bare arm slid out, and the bodies, toward the top of the mound, stiffly shifted as they were shoved aside.

A head appeared, followed by a naked chest, writhing loose.

The man struggled clear, fighting to free himself and stand at the top of the pile.

At once, he looked toward the window the commander was gazing through.

He ducked back and rolled over, staring up at the articles compressed together: a doll in a button-up dress, the corner edge of a side table, a small rug with fringes, a straw basket with a few strands broken…

While studying the articles packed around him, he understood why they might have been put into storage. They were non-essential. Austerity was the reversionary pattern used to formulate and fabricate the world he had found himself in. Simplification. Easy to understand, except for the brutality, the cruelty, which he suspected might – after all – belong to a life that lacked embellishment.

It was impossible to shift his body around in the tunnel, to rearrange his position to a head-first advantage, so he made his return on his back, edging ahead, gazing down at his boots, until they poked out the opening, and his legs bent to find the floor.

As though spring-loaded, he popped back up. Vertical and prepared.

Ahead of him lay the broken trail of articles he had dispelled.

When he reappeared in the street, the younger soldier watched him in the way the older soldier once had.

Berserk screams were coming from the bakery.

He looked that way, and was told the black-haired woman was being interrogated by the remaining officer.

"Why?" the commander asked, although he felt it might no longer be his place to enquire.

"To find the real truth," the younger soldier stated, his eyes giving nothing away, while they turned to watch down the alleyway.

The commander checked to see a grey, naked body standing there, its hands dangling by its sides, as though useless. The body watched ahead. It was trying to say something, its lips trembling. The intentions of another step, and it fell to the ground, remained lodged there on its left shoulder, its gaze level with the earth.

The younger soldier hurriedly walked to the body, and drew his revolver.

"No," said the commander, stepping nearer, for a keener look at it.

The naked man turned his eyes to gawk up at him.

"Brother," the man croaked.

The commander stared, his eyes becoming hot, his throat thickening.

The younger soldier said: "What?" He gritted his teeth. "You call him brother!"

"Brother," the man whispered again, a thirsty plea in his voice.

It was the man he had watched climb from the pile of bodies behind the remaining houses of this town, this town that had once been his, yet now seemed less and less his giving realm.

The man naked to the world.

A fate akin to his.

"Get him some water," the commander said to the younger soldier, but the younger soldier had already fired.

The shot kicked up dirt beside the naked man's chin.

The naked man opened his eyes again. A simple gesture without a trace of fright.

"Stop it," the commander said, snatching the revolver away.

"It's your own undoing then," said the younger soldier, but to which of the two men it was impossible to tell.

CHAPTER 6

"I'm sorry," said the black-haired woman. "I should have said nothing." She gently washed the face of the naked man who had come from the pile of bodies and was now settled on a narrow bed. "They did this to you."

The man watched the woman's face. It was cut at the lips and there were bruises around her eyes. The sight was a mesmerizing treasure to him. He wondered if he had played a part in it.

"It was my fault." She dipped the cloth in a pan of water, then dabbed at his dry lips. "I should have said nothing."

The naked man could not think why the black-haired woman was washing him, why she was apologizing to him of all people. He wondered what had happened to the woman's face. Was she one of them or another? A casualty of what sort? She was familiar. He could not help but imagine her with shorter hair, and a stillness in her body.

He tried not to think because it pained him.

He was glad to be alive.

None of this mattered now. The distance or difference between two peoples.

Now that he was alive, it was all a gift to him. Every movement, every moment, a miracle. This lovely woman to care for him. Her gentle, precise touch.

Out from the merciful clarity that he recognized as his life, he thought he might weep for forgiveness.

A man, changed.

He took a breath and continued studying the woman's face, the bruises, the abrasions, then lower, the welts and scars on her body. They urged something inside of him, something not so thankful.

The welts and scars reminded him that he had been shot, been in bed with a woman much like the one before him. Thankful to start anew. The bodies in the pile. He had mastered them. He had survived. He was at peace.

No, triumphant.

It was a gift to be alive, a gift that had not so much been given him as he had taken, a gift that he had achieved.

Not a gift at all, actually, but an eventuality.

Destiny.

A gift that he had given himself by surviving. Thankful for his own unfaltering will.

One of the chosen people, so why should he be surprised?

The naked woman with the long black hair.

A punished dog.

Thankful for his own doing.

Look at her, he told himself, reaching out and touching the woman's left nipple with his grey fingers. Look at that.

The woman stopped.

The naked man regarded her face. He had saved her, so that he might deal with her in private, in her home town, in front of her family. Where was her family? He would soon find out enough.

He waited, then pinched her nipple between his thumb and forefinger, the pressure swelling his fingertips pink.

The woman flinched, her touch paused. She looked more carefully at the man's face, which had taken on an expression of fierce interest.

There was a silence, before she said: "Why did you do that?"

The words sprang to his lips, as though by instinct: "For as a man thinks in his heart, so he is."

The commander, the younger soldier and the remaining officer listened to the crackling speaker, the voices of the naked man from the pile of bodies and the black-haired woman, both in the room next door.

The woman and the man had been thrown into one of the rooms above the bakery to see what might be learned from them. The familiarity with which they addressed each other seemed to validate certain suspicions.

"There's conspiracy here," vowed the remaining officer. He was eating an apple, cutting wedges away with his knife, and sliding them into his mouth. There was red smeared on the flesh of the apple, perhaps carried over from the peel.

The younger soldier listened intently, as though it might be a program on the radio, and it would be a crime to miss a single dramatic insinuation.

"He's already passed on confidential information," said the remaining officer, alertly. "Where did he get this information? How did he know?"

All eyes were on the commander, who mutely watched the speaker, for from it came an eerie voice he took to be his own.

At first, the naked man was sorry. Behind closed doors, the man told the woman that when he found himself in the pile of bodies, it had changed him. The man had cried openly for the death that had nearly claimed him. He had felt the suffering. He was thankful to be alive. He praised Elohim for granting him salvation.

"Here," said the woman, straightening the woollen

blanket around the man's shoulders, for he was trembling.

Before entering the room, the naked man had been issued a blanket as part of the conventions pertaining to wartime incarceration. The woman, not thought of as a captive, was assigned nothing.

The man's teary eyes were grateful. He considered offering the woman his blanket to conceal her nudity, yet he felt a sense of righteousness to be covered in front of her. It was with mounting interest that his eyes travelled the length of the woman's body, the weakness in him hardening with each inch of flesh discovered and personalized.

When his eyes met hers, the woman knew that an adjustment had been calculated.

The man's trembling had ceased. "I wondered how I could have ended up with the dead. I am not dead."

The naked woman gave a little smile, although the smile seemed to hurt a touch.

"The more I thought of it, the more I knew I had been wronged. I wasn't meant to be with the bodies."

"None of us are meant to be with the bodies."

The man paused to consider these words, yet they found no anchor in him. "I had been betrayed."

"Betrayed?"

"Yes, betrayed."

"By who?"

"My own brother. My twin. The man whose death I had ordered."

The woman carefully stood from where she had been helping the man.

"Ordered?" she said with trepidation.

"Yes," said the man, taking greater interest. He sat up and slid his legs over the edge of the bed. Once his soles touched the floor, he continued, "And he is something to you. I can see that now." He let the blanket slip from his shoulders, the purple erection – pole-straight and vein-hard – poked up from between his legs. "You felt sorry for me, but it was really for him, wasn't it? You and him, the same."

The woman took a step away, her eyes cast toward the door.

"I felt sorry for myself, too," said the man, standing from the mattress. "But that does no good. The life came back into me."

The woman shook her head, refusing to believe.

"Now, I almost feel sorry for you. You filthy Mu'min."

The muffled cries of the woman sounded through the speaker.

The remaining officer looked at his watch. "Twenty-seven minutes," he said, "up to this point. And each minute, he seems to grow stronger."

There came a thrusting roar through the speaker and the speech-sizzle of vile accusations that energized punishment, followed by a bellowed oath: "In the name of the Reign of Canaan."

The remaining officer and the younger soldier looked at the commander. In light of the actions in the next room, they were growing unconvinced of his capabilities.

"Listen to that," said the younger soldier, reverentially. "What is he using on her?"

"Something unwelcome, like a prying neighbour," said the remaining officer, and they both laughed while facing each other. "I expect he's inventive."

Then they both looked at the commander, their laughter turning to grins that soon vanished, faithless.

"Nothing like the story you told," announced the remaining officer.

"What?" The commander lowered the volume on the metal speaker, for the woman's cries were becoming more panicky, ragged and desperate, yet less energetic.

"What you told her last night," the remaining officer reminded him.

The commander glanced at the speaker, and realized that a similar listening device had been placed in his room.

"What were you trying to get from her using such lies?" asked the remaining officer.

By the way the two men were looking at him, he knew it was time to take action. If he did not react resolutely, in the capacity of leader, he would lose himself to the man in the other room who was presently and willingly proving himself.

Yet he could not spirit himself beyond silence. He listened to the crackle of what was being done to the woman, and it made him sombre.

Finally, he tried this: "Love is a powerful tool."

"Love?" said the remaining officer incredulously. "A tool for what?"

"Extraction."

The younger soldier watched the commander as though he might have understood, but the remaining officer was having none of it.

"And what did you extract from her?" asked the remaining officer.

"What I was trying to get from her I got." Yet despite

his attempt at a smile, a smile that was meant to be self-aggrandizing, yet felt pathetic on his lips, the two men merely studied him, suspecting a new intrigue.

CHAPTER 7

That night, after being watched for the remainder of the day by the wary eyes of those once under his command, he retired early to his room in hopes of devising a strategy.

He had just come from the holding cell in the bakery, where the naked man had been taken after treating the woman with such violence.

"I believe it might be best to keep him alive," the remaining officer had suggested, tipping his chin toward the naked, pacing prisoner in the cell, "until we confirm his identity. He put on a good show, but how much of it was truly from the heart?"

"You know who he says he is," the commander had countered, his voice unsteady, as though being leached from him.

"You know who I am," the naked man shouted at the top of his lungs.

"Yes," replied the remaining officer, brandishing an odious smile at the commander. "You, sir."

While walking away, he regretted not having shot the remaining officer. The act would have been a potent and, perhaps, pleasing diversion but – ultimately – would have done him no good. He would then have had to shoot the younger soldier and whoever else passed through town to hear the ravings of the man in the holding cell.

The only act of certainty would be to shoot the prisoner, but that would cast further suspicion on him, and the man – once disposed of – might merely crawl from the pile of bodies again. Stronger, more resolved.

The commander's thoughts were troubled by all of this as he entered his room with his eyes on the floorboards. Looking up, he noticed a foreign bulk in his bed, the long, grey hair and the thickness of the female form. He came to a standstill, his hand on the doorknob.

At once, he glanced around the room, trying to divine the hiding place of the listening device. He assumed the overhead light fixture or the lamp on the bedside table.

"Hello," he said, the word coming from him without reflection.

The grey-haired woman on the bed did not stir.

Shutting the door, he concluded that this was meant to be a test. No, more than a test… a contest.

In another room, identical to this one, the prisoner might have been placed in a duplicate situation, his actions recorded and weighed against the commander's actions.

The trick was for one of them to outdo the other.

With his eyes on the naked old woman, he heard loud

footsteps beyond his door. No secret effort was being made to conceal their presence.

The footsteps came to a standstill directly outside his room.

He expected a knock, but it never came. There were no voices, no mutterings or whispers, only the occasional rustle of movement.

He sat on the edge of the bed with his back to the old woman, his eyes on the door, on the hook three-quarters of the way up. He stood and removed his long coat, carefully hung it on the hook.

Returning to the bed, he kept his eyes off the old woman and sat. He bounced a little to make the bedsprings creek. Conscious of the men beyond his door, he increased the momentum of his bounce. He breathed through his open mouth, made his breath an audible rasping, then snorted through his nostrils and came up with the expected sound of gratification.

He muttered, "Filthy Mu'min," under his breath, half-heartedly mimicking what he had heard. "In the name of..."

What if they come in, he thought.

Standing, he quickly unbuckled his belt, pulled down his trousers, and looked back at the old woman. Her hair was spread out along the pillow. It was not entirely grey, as he first suspected, but had streaks of black throughout. Who was this old woman? He could not tell by her face, for it had a wrinkled complexion that made her features indistinct. How long had she been dead? Her skin was grey with tinges of green towards the extremities. And what was this old woman to him?

Just then there came a rap on the door.

He flinched.

"Commander?" asked a voice.

"Come in," he said as he hurriedly reached down to pull up his trousers.

The remaining officer entered, followed by the younger soldier, who led the naked man into the room. The prisoner was no longer naked, but dressed in black pants and a shirt, and – most damning of all – his hands were not bound.

The commander locked eyes with the prisoner.

The prisoner showed no sign of respect or remorse, but shook his head in a chastising manner, then gazed at the old woman on the bed, his entire being seeming to seep that way.

This will be it, the commander told himself, while buckling his belt. This will prove who we are.

Brushing past the commander, the prisoner went to the far side of the bed, and reached down between the old woman's legs, probing roughly and without feeling.

"Dry," said the prisoner, the word like a stab directed at the commander.

The younger soldier and the remaining officer watched the commander, then shifted their eyes to the bed upon hearing the sound of a blow being delivered.

No cry came in return, only one creaking bounce of the bedsprings.

The prisoner muttered accusations, before a second meatier blow sounded, followed by a slap. There was a moment of silence as the prisoner seemed to struggle with dead weight.

Then came the shredding of cloth.

At this point, the commander could not prevent himself from glancing back, for the old woman on the bed had been naked.

The prisoner had taken off his shirt and was tearing strips from it. With two of the strips, he secured each of the old woman's hands to the rungs of the iron headboard.

The commander looked away, toward the open door, where he expected others to enter, to linger, to watch in revelation.

Why bind the arms of a dead woman?

Behind him, the bedsprings creaked, as weight was added atop weight.

Another blow sounded and then another, each one increasing in vigour and punctuated by vulgar words, as the bounce of the bedsprings became a more extreme riot.

The iron headboard thudded into the wall.

Up on the ceiling, the light fixture swayed.

The bedside lamp fell over and smashed.

The commander thought of hoof beats, storming towards them across miles of desert. A jihad fast approaching.

As the thrusting increased, sprinkles of plaster drifted down from the ceiling, flecking the three men in the room.

More and more, the headboard pounded into the wall, until it was raining dust.

The commander became aware of his hands. They were growing warm. He had no idea where to put them.

With eyes fixed on the bed, the younger soldier and the remaining officer quietly backed away, their expressions made rigid by the intensity of the scene, until they were safely standing in the doorway.

At that point, at the first sound of cartilage being

crushed, they both looked away, one to the left, the other to the right.

And at a later point – at the sound of bone splintering – they stole one glance back, and were compelled to shut the door to mute the demonstration.

The commander stood still. At his back, the silent endurance of the old woman, the submissive pleading of the black-haired bakery worker, and – ultimately, toward the beginning where the prisoner came alertly to attention then bowed out – the secretive whisperings of the little girl who – tucked away in her hiding place beneath the floorboards – refused to expire.

CHAPTER 8

A message was coming in behind the new commander. He waited for the machine to stop and then read the two words printed on the strip of paper: "Conflict over." Followed by the name of the Supreme Commander.

The new commander tore off the strip and brought it to the prisoner in the holding cell at the back of the bakery.

As the new commander approached the makeshift cell, the younger soldier – who had been guarding the prisoner – came to full attention.

"Conflict over," the new commander announced, repeating the words that had been sent to him through the telewire.

The prisoner quietly looked up from his bunk to see the younger soldier smile. It was a good-natured smile. A smile that had gone missing. He was just a boy, after all.

The boy went to the new commander and offered his hand, but the commander kept his eyes trained on the prisoner.

"So, you have won?" asked the prisoner.

The new commander looked down at the strip. He read the words again.

More noise from the telewire. This outburst even briefer.

The new commander strode to the machine and tore off the strip, read the single word there: "Evacuate."

The soldiers would be relieved now. Returned to their homes in the various regions beyond these borders, they would sleep in beds with their benevolent wives and kiss their fortunate children good morning.

Families would be reunited.

The men would return to their jobs, to take up tools, to fix and build.

Or would they?

The new commander looked toward the window.

The conflict was over.

What did it mean?

He listened. A feeling in the soles of his boots cut short his breath. The far-off rumble of something grave approaching.

All these days, while he sat in his cell, the prisoner had wondered why the new commander had not called for his extermination. Perhaps the new commander had heard rumours of the impending end of the conflict.

Perhaps, when all was said and done, they were brothers, and would now be brothers again.

The new commander watched the prisoner, then instructed the younger soldier to leave them in peace.

The younger soldier glanced at the prisoner, smiling to share his new fortune, to wish him nothing but the very best, then made his way from the room.

Watching the younger soldier go, the prisoner saw how it would be: in seven days, filthy and battered, and having escaped a number of skirmishes by the skin of his teeth, refusing to surrender on his way to his home for one final look at his mutilated mother, the younger soldier would be shot through the head in the street.

Once the door had closed, the new commander said, as though he had been saving the words up for as long as they had lived: "You remember when we were children, that time you tried to save me from the tiger?"

The prisoner nodded, thinking that now might be the time to smile at the recollection, yet the emotion could not be made absolute. Instead, he watched his hands where they dangled between his knees. "It was only an imaginary tiger," he conceded.

"No. A tiger with an eagle perched on its back. Remember? You hated it so, but I loved the look of it."

"It was only an imaginary tiger. You dreamt of it."

"Yes, but not imaginary." The new commander drew his revolver. "You tried to take that tiger from me. It was too dangerous, you said."

"All it wanted was to eat you up."

"Yes, but I let it anyway." The new commander raised the revolver, levelling it. "And here we are, which one of us a skeleton?"

The prisoner shrugged.

"I've already exterminated the remaining officer, as you were meant to do. The younger soldier is your only hope now."

The prisoner stared at the new commander, wondering what he might do next, for it seemed as though he had lost something of his signature confidence.

"Yes, we, the Twelve Tribes, have settled the conflict," the new commander proudly pledged, yet with a lying quaver in his voice. "Finally. Our land conquered."

"So, what need is there for me now," admitted the prisoner, blandly watching the revolver. He thought of rising from the edge of his bunk, but could not summon the resolve. He had been without spirit for quite some time. "There is only need of you."

The new commander raised the revolver, and placed the tip against his own temple. "I believe the opposite is true."

The prisoner stood, his mind no longer a blank.

"What good is there now? To rot in peace. When the

eagle rises from the tiger's back to screech 'Shalom,' it sounds like this." And the new commander fired.

CHAPTER 9

That night, there were inexplicable sounds. The direction of the distant, barely discernible tones shifted from east to west, as though his ears were playing tricks on him, or the wind was constantly changing direction, although there was not a trace of breeze.

From his view through the bars, he stared out into the black night. As much as he strained to search in both directions, he could not spot a fire.

The sounds came like whispers from a dream a hundred kilometres off. A hint of something, a rumble in the earth, and then nothing, so that he thought it might be his mind throwing up distractions.

In the morning, the sounds were more distinct, although they remained fleeting and evasive. Regardless, there was a crowding in his head.

During the night, he had heard not a peep in the room, yet as the light showed itself, he saw that the body of the new commander had vanished. He searched around inside himself, yet could find it nowhere.

Activity beyond his cell took on a more energetic stride, as though the once distant, fleeting and evasive sounds were now spurring on a local call to action.

The younger soldier entered, his hand remaining on

the door, while he cast a wary look over the cell. Then, he left, only to return some time later. It was peculiar to watch. The younger soldier staring into the cell, then back over his shoulder, dubious of resolution, weighing what might matter.

The distant noises were not so vague now. What could be heard most prominently were machine sounds and what he thought might have been hoof beats, horses. The muted, yet sustained, shouting of men.

Opened mouths bounding nearer, through a wavering haze.

As he lay in darkness, he heard the wall of noise prod out individual sounds. The noises became dissimilar and individual, like a map with mountain ranges being punched into definition. The land was crossed, the space occupied, no longer separating.

He stood at his window and watched out into darkness. There was noise straight ahead of him, yet he could see nothing under the moon-absent sky.

Darkness made of sound, closing in.

How far away was it? he wondered.

There was not a glimmer of light, not a hint of muted metal, not a stain of fire. The nearing sounds were as indefinite as vapour, yet his ears caught the intermittent crests of them.

As the red spread through the sky, he saw that the horizon was no longer a blank line but set with the darker outline of small figures. Single-mindedly conceived, it was all farther away than he suspected, yet stampeding straight at him.

He woke to the roar of movement blasting to crescendo: the grinding percussion of engines, the grating and heavy squeaking of tank tracks, the rumble of hoof beats, the shouts of men.

All of it stilling a moment after he opened his eyes.

He sat up on his bunk.

Engines being shut off, the whinnying of horses. The sounds clarified as voices, boot steps, booming directives…

The younger soldier entered with an officer who was identified as the troop leader of the American coalition forces.

"And this is the man?" asked the troop leader, his blond hair slicked back, his blue uniform clean, impeccably tailored, and matching the colour of his eyes, the star emblem affixed above his left breast. "Why hasn't he been transported? He might be of profit to us in the exchange program."

"We don't know who he is, sir."

"Give me his file." The troop leader shot out his black-gloved hand, while he curtly examined the prisoner.

The younger soldier went to the cabinet and returned with the file.

"Go," said the troop leader, snatching the file.

The younger soldier left.

At once, the troop leader sat at the desk, and read through the papers. Occasionally, he glanced over with interest at the prisoner. When he was done, he shut the file, and stood.

"This makes nothing obvious," the troop leader announced through the bars. "It seems you had a brother. One of you is dead. So which one do you claim to be?"

Wordlessly, the prisoner watched the troop leader drop a cigarette to the floor, and smear the life from it with his boot heel. There seemed to be nothing left to say, for the troop leader departed without notice.

A few minutes later, the troop leader returned with the black-haired woman from the bakery.

"What choice of interrogation methods were employed

here?" asked the leader, tilting his head toward the woman. "You saw to her."

The woman whimpered and watched him, turning her slow, swollen eyes to the ground. Her naked wrists were bound behind her back. Her hair had been snipped short.

"She is nothing to you then," said the troop leader.

The prisoner watched the woman. She was someone he thought he might have helped. Someone he might have loved if he could only convince himself.

The troop leader drew his revolver. By the expression on his face, his gestures became more meaningful as he gradually levelled the revolver to the woman's temple.

"Are you a Mu'min, one of the chosen, or what exactly?" the troop leader asked in a tight voice.

The prisoner had no idea. If it was in his heart where he was meant to search, he found nothing there but a slot.

The leader glanced at the woman's sobbing, disfigured face, her eyes still cast down, knowing better.

"She keeps her eyes away from you, as though you are her superior. Of course, you might very well be." The troop leader looked from the woman to him, then back to the woman, finding encouragement. "Or is it simply shame?" And he fired the gun, the impact – snapping the woman's head to the side – splintered bone, and raised her eyes to him for one final look as she tilted to the ground. She fell without restriction, her wrists secured behind her back.

It took a while for the sound of the gunshot and the pounding of weight against the floorboards to settle.

Now, the revolver was turned on him.

"Her God did nothing to save her. But you. What are you?"

He said not a word in his defence. It was impossible.

"You must know," the troop leader demanded. "How could you not know? Tell me."

"I have no memory of it."

"Memory?" The American troop leader held the revolver aimed steadily between a space in the bars, the tip of the barrel framed in iron. "Memory has nothing to do with admission." His eyes shifted uncertainly, as though a thought had come over him. "If you are a commander then you were educated, trained. You would know the tenets of the Six One Three."

He said nothing.

"Within the Six One Three, which tenet are you? Which number?"

The prisoner gave a feeble shake of his head.

"No? Perhaps a chant then, a string of Allah Akbars."

Nothing.

"One or the other," demanded the troop leader. "We have little time here."

The troop leader watched through the bars. He waited. Then he glanced back at the file on the desk. As though in a fury, he holstered his revolver and strode toward the desk. He seized the file in both hands and tore it to shreds.

"Let them figure you out," he said. Then he stormed from the room, the door banging shut on its coil hinges.

Some time later, the door opened and two soldiers, unknown to him, removed the filing cabinet.

The prisoner waited but no one else came to see him. He stared at the naked dead woman on the floor. She had worked in the bakery. He remembered the sweet smell of her when they were close.

A black-red finger of blood crept toward him from a larger pool. He waited until it was almost too late, then moved his bare feet away.

As time went on, it became dark and the flies arrived through the bars in his window to investigate.

From the sounds that reached him, he could tell that items were being hastily packed away in trucks.

There was much activity and voices curtly giving

instruction. People were being moved. The noise was heading off, one section at a time.

As light from the yellow crescent moon came in through his window, he listened to hear complete silence.

Not one human sound could be discerned.

The others had left.

He perceived the stillness with physical acuity, as though his entire body was sensing impoverishment or relief.

Yet when he bowed his head, and shut his eyes in concentration, he sensed the tremor of another army charging nearer, across the earth. A force that the fleeing had denied, yet feared.

The flies did not ever sleep.

He sat on the bed and waited.

The odour from the front of his cell drifted to him as the sun began to brighten what lay beyond the bars.

His lips grew dry from breathing through his mouth.

There was no way to escape the smell.

He stood and went to the pail of water on the floor at the foot of his bunk. Squatting, he kept his eyes fixed on the grey wall, and sipped what he took to be his rationed allotment, knowing that he must preserve what little water remained.

He would not use the water to clean up the blood that thickened and blackened near his feet.

He moved the pail away from where it was set, and placed it in the far corner. Then he took off his shirt and covered the pail to prevent the flies from polluting it.

Darkness came again. Creatures entered between the window bars, and crept down the wall to slink or scurry across the floor.

From where he sat on his bed, he watched them move as shadows, his eyes following their trails toward the taller bars where they freely slipped through.

Nothing could prevent them from mounting their claim, from taking the woman's flesh as their own.

In the daylight, they had disappeared, their snorting, lapping and chewing noises gone with them.

The stench clashed with his hunger until his hunger was removed, and it was night again.

The stench drew larger creatures that passed before him in the darkness, going one way, then the other, one occasionally pausing to raise its head and make a threatening noise at another.

Bugs appeared of every conceivable shape and colour. Yellow and green. Red and brown. Blue and orange. Some with wings that allowed them to fly short distances only.

There were ants everywhere, climbing, circling, progressing in orderly lines. Blindly, they worked in concert, for the common good of their ranks.

CHAPTER 10

He was astonished by the speed with which a body could be stripped of flesh. So many living things with such urgent need. What would they be eating otherwise? he wondered. What was no longer famished because of this?

Shouldn't death be everywhere?

And then he realized that it was.

Hysteria made him chuckle.

One feeding from the other, he thought, and the other feeding from the first, yet neither of the same flesh.

A domesticated dog with a name, a homeless dog without one. No contest in choosing the one to be shot first.

When there was nothing but polished bone left of the woman, his mind decided for him. He knew who he was and who he was not. He raised the water pail and looked down into it. There was an eighth of a litre remaining.

How far would that get him in the confines of his cell?

In awe, he slowly turned over the pail, allowed the remnants to run and trickle onto the dried blood.

The spill was a disburdening relief that mollified his body.

It only took water to make the blood flow again.

He felt it seep around his toes, soak into his skin to rise along the edges of his soles.

These are my stained feet, he heard himself say. *And it has not been a comfortable sleep with her.*

He moved his eyes toward the bones that faced the ceiling.

Where his feet had been stuck to the floor, they came away with a viscous sound, as he knelt in submission and lowered his lips.

The sound of his kiss was the lock on his door released.